THE G̶R̶ BRIDGE

Eddy Murray

Published in Belfast by Shanway Press

ISBN: 978-0-9566885-8-3

Email: info@shanway.com
           amdaenv@gmail.com

Category: Fiction
           Ireland

Title: The Green Bridge

Author: Eddy Murray

©Shanway press

THE GREEN BRIDGE

Eddy Murray

Dedication

This story is dedicated to Mary.

'Cast a cold eye on life, on death.
Horseman pass by'

W.B. Yeats

Eddy Murray

Eddy Murray

contents

Eddy Murray

1 PROLOGUE

Historical background

Jim Sweeney first saw daylight in 1949 when he opened his eyes in the Irish state, itself only twenty eight years old. He lived his early life in a free state of childhood bliss in Donegal beside the Lackan river and experienced twenty seven years in this vale of tears before his final departure. The Lackan is a minor salmon river of Ireland which rises in the Lough of the same name. This was the territory of Niall Garbh O'Donnell in the reign of Elizabeth I; he was the rival to Red Hugh O'Donnell and in the end helped the English to defeat him. However, after Niall was no longer needed, the English threw him into the Tower of London. They left him there, without being charged, for 15 years until he died in 1626.

The main topographical feature of the countryside is the many drumlins which were deposited by the glacier in the last ice age 10,000 years before and now shelter the village called Ballyjordan from the north-western wind. This name is derived from the Irish language and means the town of the horsetail ferns. The village and neighbouring parishes are associated forever with the glorious name of the republican martyr, O'Donnell. The O'Donnell family farm house is preserved as a part of the national heritage in grateful memory of the man who was a leading supporter of the document called the 1916 proclamation of independence or the proclamation of Ireland as the property of the Irish people. He escaped execution by gunshot for engaging in the 1916 rising, was active in the war of independence but was killed in the civil war that followed.

Rain bearing clouds, carrying evaporated water from the Atlantic Ocean, rise across the Sligo, Leitrim and Donegal mountains before being carried inland by the western wind and spilling their surplus moisture onto rainy glens on eastern slopes. This water is brought to the lough and river Lackan through land drains that traverse many hilly and rushy townlands with names like Cloonlough, Maghanlawaun, Derrykeevan, Aghoo, Clontuskett, Lisnagarvey, Tawnyunshinagh, Lughawnagh, Magheravelly, Cornafannoge, Moneenlom, Ardlougher and Stranoodan. Meaningful place names describing some characteristic of the area which will soon recede in local consciousness as will the memory of the humans who determined them. These will be lost connections in Ireland like those of forgotten peoples such as the Arapahoe, Seminole or Sioux Native Americans that some of the dispossessed people of Ireland or their descendants were active in displacing seventy years earlier.

Many Irish, who were fleeing the famine or just general poverty, went to America where they joined the US army, probably as a source of employment. Thousands of them served and died with distinction, on both sides, in the American civil war that ended in 1865. In due course, and inevitably, many of the survivors became involved in the war against the native inhabitants and the land grab that followed. Notable examples who survived the civil war were Sheridan whose people came from the Ulster area and Meagher, the Young Irelander, who came from Waterford. Generals Sheridan and Meagher were famous 'Indian' fighters who were also, paradoxically, the first to raise awareness of the beauty of unspoilt nature in those parts. For example they introduced the revolutionary idea of preserving areas of wilderness and were instrumental in setting up Yellowstone National Park. Meagher's role in the American civil war was mentioned by JFK when he addressed both houses of the Irish Government during his 1963 visit. There was no reference to Meagher's post war activities. General Sheridan is mentioned in John Ford's last western- Cheyenne Autumn.

The Lackan river water cuts its way through the land and eventually arrives at the upper reaches of the Foyle from where it travels back via this tidal river to the ocean - the often cursed cycle of water that continues quietly and forever through the local life and countryside, changing and creating the people and the landscape.

The Irish peasant people have little connection with the waterways of Ireland or its associated flora and fauna. Perhaps this is a legacy of history because the landless and dispossessed were not allowed to take fish from the waters or birds from the estates of the local landlord. He lived in The Big House and his ownership had been established by various acts and legal instruments of the English parliament going back as far as Cromwell, the arch-republican who 'toured' Ireland from 1649-1653. During the time of Cromwell it must be noted that most Irish Catholics had allegiance to the royalist cause. They were the loyalists of their day.

The Irish government and its many civil servants have the same role now where the salmon rivers are concerned. In any case there were few fish caught or eaten in South Donegal during the great famine when the native population was starved and nearly wiped out. It has still not recovered and the stunned survivors were soon re-immersed in sullen acceptance of a God-fearing, impoverished existence. The men developed a culture of escape into alcohol, the women into religion.

Donegal is a fine example of the forgotten Ireland in the fifty years of the 20th century since the proclamation of independence in 1916 and its partial achievement in 1922. Proclamations rarely succeed in freeing people from the hardships of poverty but do succeed in providing many opportunities for charlatan politicians. Nor are the poor ever free from the fear that comes to them and their children from religious faith. Generations of small farmers and their wives with a few cows and many children lived out a precarious existence on thin soil and were accustomed to emigration.

The dance hall called the Red Barn in the Bronx would be as well known to some of the people of South Donegal as their own local Dreamland Ballroom at the crossroads in Glenlackan village which is exactly half way between the small towns of Tirmore and Ballyleagh. The ballroom was the only light shining in the area and had started its romantic life as a humble corrugated shed in 1934 when a courageous, returning native from the USA called John McGurn decided he was going to don a bow tie and become a dancehall promoter. To say the only light in the local area is not quite true because there was also the light of the Holy Spirit, the light of love from Jesus represented by the red sanctuary lamp that shone out as a fearsome beacon of hope in the chapel. It could be argued that the lamp and religion itself was at least a useful reminder of something sacred in the world to contrast with the often nasty and brutish experience of material life.

The, ever hopeful, small farmer raised his cattle to feed the food market in Britain and his children to feed the labour markets in Britain and America. There was a standing joke amongst holidaying yanks, especially second generation ones who were not bound by the loyalties of direct family ties, that the first thing an Irish small farmer would do was take the visitor out to view his tiny cattle herd. It was easy to understand this pride in his cattle and land because the peasant Irish generation in the first half of the twentieth century still had living memories of the famine and strong folklore recounting the state of the catholic before emancipation when, for example, a catholic could not own a horse worth more than five pounds. If he did own such an animal the law said that any protestant could buy it for his own price without appeal.

The famous Irish language poem, Caoineadh Airt Ui Laoghaire - A lament for Art O'Leary - tells the story. It was written by Eileen O'Connell who is, understandably, very upset because her beloved husband had been shot dead. Art had refused to comply with the wishes of a protestant man called Morris who desired to possess his horse. In the poem the grieving woman is full of frustration and hatred. She cries out for revenge and justice.

The only real survivor in the South Donegal area was the politician, the small business man, the pub owner, the cattle dealer, the auctioneer, the grocer, the funeral undertaker, the teacher and the doctor who was on a par with the priest. The solicitor and the banker lived a separate life in the town of Ballyleagh and were consulted only in cases of extreme need or the lunatic pursuit of some legal judgement. One person often adopted or inherited several of the local business roles to serve the people and enrich himself. The children of these business or professional people got sent away for an education to return as the doctors and teachers of the locality. Emigration was not for them and of course not for the politician's child either. Politicians unashamedly appeared at election time to open – to open anything – a new road scheme that took a bend out of the road, a new restaurant, a rare new factory or maybe to judge some local enterprise such as a pike, perch, trout or salmon fishing competition.

So life went on and the Dreamland ballroom flourished as the only venue for local experimentation with the rituals of the mating game which was always held in check by the Episcopal gaze. Quite how one was supposed to even think about making love with a temple of the Holy Ghost was and remains a real mystery. The bishops had long decreed that no dances would be held in Ireland during Lent, the 40 days of penance leading up to the triumph of Easter. During this period the show bands went to England or America to play to the emigrants in drinking clubs like the Four Seasons or the Garryowen in Birmingham, The Galtymore in Cricklewood or the Red Barn in the Bronx. These were grandly called tours of Britain and the U.S. by bands with names like The Miami, The Drifters, The Mainliners, The Mighty Avons or The Royal.

Glenlackan was a mile or two from the border depending on the road taken. It was also only a few miles from Ballyjordan village and therefore it too had a close association with O'Donnell, the republican martyr. This had caused a culture of old style republicanism, with its single article of faith, to diffuse into the local soul where it persists today. The article of republican faith states that the Irish border divides Ireland and forces six of the thirty two counties to remain under British rule which is an offence against the moral, physical, mental, economic and political health of all the people on the island and therefore has to go. Every so often the IRA started and will start a campaign of shooting and bombing against the British forces of occupation and their local Unionist allies who took up arms to defend the border and their cash cow, Britain. The familiar litany of the campaign years, which were always called the troubles, stretched all the way back to 1922 -1940, 1956, 1963, and 1969. The usual salutation and correct procedure in Ireland when one meets a bereaved person is to shake the hand of the afflicted while saying 'Sorry for your troubles'.

The modern era

In 1976 the latest and longest campaign of the 20th century was underway and had not even reached half time. It was different this time because it was organic and home grown. It was a violent spin off from the civil rights movement which itself had been germinated by newly educated Catholics, fed by awareness of blatant discrimination in the six counties and modelled on Martin Luther King's non-violent campaign in the US. So this time it had not entered the northern nationalist consciousness via the border but had started in Belfast and Derry before spreading to the borderlands and rural areas. There were retrospective suspicions that the English were initially behind the whole provisional IRA thing, possibly because they wanted to be out of Ireland and certainly because they wanted an end of the civil rights campaign which they could not control. Whatever about the origins of the campaign of violence, things got out of hand with bombings, shootings and deaths common along the border and throughout the six counties. One incident was to have a direct impact upon the life of Jim Sweeney.

A newspaper report gave the simple facts. On 15 August 1975, Harry Hill (20), Richard Evans (39) and Thomas Bowls (36), all members of the Royal Ulster Constabulary (RUC), were killed in a Provisional Irish Republican Army land mine attack on their foot patrol searching a field near Strancally RUC base. Strancally is in the six counties and on the border across from Tirmore in Donegal which in turn is a few mile down the road from Glenlackan. The IRA simply fired some shots in a field behind the police barracks in the night. At first light a search was organised with the full barrack force of police and army combing the fields for spent bullets. The ensuing landmine explosion claimed the lives of the three policemen and was either set off by someone watching at the end of a command wire or by a trip wire triggered by the victims.

The British army reacted immediately and blew up a few more minor roads across the border and also the green bridge which was a disused railway bridge near Tirmore. This had carried the Strancally to Ballyleagh railway on a single track which closed in 1959. The rails and rolling stock were sold to Pakistan. For some reason the green bridge, so called because of its green oxide anti-rust coating, was left in place and indeed one could still cross its metal girders on foot into Northern Ireland. Some British security expert must have identified the disused bridge as a possible entry point for the recent bomb. A child could see that this was an extremely unlikely route for delivery of a bomb into Tyrone so the logic of this British vandalism was difficult to see. The local people on both sides of the border thought it was simply a vindictive display of power to show that the British forces also had explosives and that something was being done to stop the terrorists.

The British army sappers attached their explosive device to the centre of the bridge span which, with its back broken, fell into the river where it remains to this day. On the day of the demolition, windows in nearby Tirmore were broken by the air percussion which was an intended or unintended outcome. The remains of the green bridge lying in the river are a memorial to all the dead and the death visited on Ireland by the line called the border. A broken backed symbol of failure imposed on Ireland and all the people in Ireland by the English ruling class who, as usual in such affairs, knew exactly what they were doing. But these matters need not concern us further here other than to say that it is not often realised that amongst the real losers from the drawing of the border were the Protestants of every denomination on the island of Ireland.

A progressive and, sometimes, revolutionary people were permanently split and turned into an unattractive, reactionary rump in Irish and world affairs. Surely England must be pleased with the outcome which forever removed a real political threat from this troublesome, neighbouring island. The native catholic Irish never did pose much of a sustained political problem ever since the time of the O'Neills, several centuries earlier. They had demonstrated a consistent pattern of behaviour whereby they would cut each other's throats as quickly as those of the enemy. History shows that many of the catholic Irish   could be easily bought and turned unlike the 'prods'.

It was long held that the Dublin government was opposed to the border and would turn a blind eye to the 'boys' who were taking direct action. This erroneous notion was certainly alive in the mind and culture of the peasant people of Ireland and was especially true of those living along the border. These rusting, romantic republican notions were repolished and transferred down the years in songs and poems that told the story of the redcoats, the British oppression and torture and the heroes who took up arms to defend the people and remove the oppressor from the island. The words and tunes of these songs are well known amongst the Irish worldwide. There were songs like Boolavogue where Fr Murphy led the people in 1798, The Bold Robert Emmet, multiple Wolfe Tone tributes including Bodenstown Churchyard, The Mountains of Pomeroy, Kevin Barry, The Ballad of James Connolly, Sean Sabhat of Garyowen in 1956 and many, many more such vehicles to keep all the patriot memories alive in the Irish heart.

In reality, the Dublin government and political classes were in the business of protecting their own private money and power machine called the Irish

Republic so it was not about to let a bunch of gunmen take over. The border and associated civil war was always there in the background and DeValera in his time, despite his republican credentials and those of his Fianna Fail 'soldiers of destiny' party, executed IRA men when it suited him. 'Sure everyone knows he was not a proper Irish man. Was he not just a cruel, sneaky, neurotic, power hungry, altar rail munching, Irish speaking, thieving, Spanish American so what would you expect?'

Things had changed by 1973 and the proper freestaters called Fine Gael were in a power coalition with labour. These were the original anti-republicans who had initially agreed to the reality of the border in 1922. One labour party chap was called Conor Cruise O'Brien and he was the appointed minister for posts and telegraphs in the coalition government. O'Brien was vehemently opposed to the provisional IRA and, to frustrate their drive to power, introduced an amendment to section 31 of the Irish broadcasting act. This piece of legislation caused eyebrows to be raised in Britain where such legislation could never have been allowed because it was so extreme, so undemocratic and so typical of a state with disciplinary tendencies.

Its introduction in Ireland again raised the question about the character of the universal Catholic. Has the catholic character some inherent flaw which makes them susceptible to such undemocratic tendencies with a willingness to implement and to accept, without question, externally applied discipline from autocratic power mongers? Is there a character or social defect which allows the catholic to consider fascism an acceptable form of government?

In any case the amendment to the broadcasting act came into force and denied republicans all access to radio or television in the twenty six counties of Ireland. The immediate effect was counterproductive but, in the longer term, it did succeed in creating a significant and permanent cultural change. It removed all the patriot songs from the broadcast media and consigned them to late night drinking sessions which are usually in Britain but can also be found further afield and indeed anywhere in the world wherever three or more drinking Irish males are gathered together. However, it is quite likely that this is the last generation capable of delivering this cultural idiom as the words of the songs are fading from popular folklore.

O'Brien was supposed to be the embodiment of a towering intellect with a matching international reputation in literary and political circles. For example he was the United Nations' representative in the Congo in the sixties and the story in Ireland at the time was that he had done a great job there. In fact it appears he was a disaster and had singlehandedly helped to foment a civil war with ongoing legacies to this day, not least for the families of young Irish soldiers killed there while on UN peacekeeping duty.

Shortly after the Strancally bomb outrage the British whispered in the, ever eager, ear of the Irish government that it must set about taking measures to defend and secure the border. Between them they agreed to set up permanent road checks on all major crossings along the border and to recrater the minor roads which the locals kept filling in. Security at the Tirmore crossing into the six counties became the responsibility of the Irish government. The Irish state authorities set up a permanent, sandbagged, army checkpoint in the middle of the town.

To make sure there were no objections from the Tirmore locals they first took the precaution of planting a car bomb in the town. This was one of those little tricks that the Irish government had picked up from their past masters in England. The Irish army defused it in a controlled explosion and 'saved' the town and its inhabitants from total destruction. After that event everyone was very glad of the protection offered by the Irish army and gardai saturating the area.

In Dublin city, paranoid anxiety filled the government and they set about protecting the politicians who were enabling this anti-republican British policy - as seen by republicans. For example the windows in the engineering department of UCD (University College Dublin) in Merrion Street overlooked the yard of Leinster House which housed the Dail - The Irish parliament. These windows posed a security risk and so were welded shut and covered with metal grids in case a sniper might be tempted to take a shot at one of the, collaborationist, Irish politicians walking in the courtyard of government buildings below.

This was Dublin and Ireland in the winter of 1976/7; a time and place of desolation, cold rain and dark evenings with a Mr and Mrs Murray on death row waiting to be hanged. The Murrays were anarchists who were involved in a bank robbery where a garda was shot and killed. Their impending hanging, later commuted by the incoming government, had enhanced the sense of depression and tragic doom in the country. The economy was also underperforming.

The election of May 1977 swept the Fine Gael coalition from power to be replaced by Jack Lynch who won a landslide election victory thanks in part to manifesto promises of general tax reduction including the removal of domestic rates and car road tax.

What Jack and his advisers did not seem to realise was that the outgoing government was so very, very unpopular and despised across the country that Beelzebub himself could have lead a political party and won. They had so enervated the population that Fianna Fail could have swept the country without any of the giveaway promises and tax reduction which has had extremely damaging consequences for the Irish economy since that time. Replacing an unpopular government was easy but it would take many years to remove the culture of fear engendered by their policies.

The UCD building in Merrion Street beside the Dail was a typically grand old colonial building whose construction in 1905 and completion in 1922 required the controversial demolition of a row of fine Georgian houses. This example of, sub-grandiose, imperial architecture was constructed in Portland stone and local granite. Presciently, in the light of later events, the building was set back behind high gates and boundary fences in case the natives got troublesome to the point of action. The building was the last British construction in colonial Ireland.

The incoming Irish politicians in the early days of the state were cute enough to realise that it would not look good for an Irish government to be located in a building with such colonial associations and appearance. Therefore it was used as a university building and housed the engineering departments until a certain Charles J. Haughey came along in the eighties with impeccable republican credentials and decided it would be a grand place for him to parade his power. His predecessor, Garret the Good, first mooted the idea but it was C.J. who sold another few Georgian houses, owned by the government, to raise the seventeen million punts needed to effect the transition. He moved the university, including the engineering department, from Dublin city centre to an awful, concreted place called Belfield and set about transforming the erstwhile colonial construction into a government building where his Irish friends and visiting dignitaries could be suitably entertained and impressed. It was encouraging to see that Irish politicians were at last starting to mature and realise it was perfectly acceptable to openly display what holding power was really about.

The visitor to Dublin can now get a free tour of the building around midday on Saturdays. The tours occur every hour on the half hour and include the Taoiseach's office and Government Cabinet room. This is one positive legacy from the late C.J. Haughey who also added a modest and tasteful fountain at the entrance which could be considered out of keeping with his otherwise flamboyant character.

So, in the interests of border security, it came to pass in 1976/77 that one hundred and forty civil gardai, backed up by an equal number of the Irish army, manned the permanent checkpoint in Tirmore and patrolled the local roads along the border. They were billeted in local houses which brought a bit of money into the area.

The Garda Siochana - Guardians of peace - The Irish Police Service.

Long before any troubles, the graduating garda recruit in the training centre at Templemore, Co Tipperary saw a border posting, especially to places like Tirmore, as the Death Valley assignment. So now, many more young and unhappy gardai from Dublin, Cork or any county might receive the unwelcome assignment news and be found on the dark border roads on a winter's night. They had lots of overtime and money so all they could do was drink in their free time and dream of getting back to civilisation. To get back to Dublin or some town where they could invest their large salaries, including the generous overtime bounty, in the housing rental market. This was the big dream followed by retirement at 50.

 Such a man was Dubliner, Garda Mc Grath who for some unknown reason had acquired Miklan as his nick name. He hated the job, the area and the local 'culchies'. He knew or believed they hated him because these border peasants and mountainy men often had old style republican notions. They always said he was there to protect the border and the British presence on the other side of it.

Eddy Murray

Miklan kept himself busy and was soon annoying local people. No dog went unchecked for licensing or car for tyre tread. However if there was one area where he excelled it was in pub watching. No late night, illegal drinking would be tolerated on his watch. Jim Sweeney first came to his attention because Miklan thought he saw him smirking in a derisory manner when he tried to clear the late night drinkers out of Keenan's pub in Glenlackan the previous week. However, the primary and technical reason for Garda McGrath's interest in Jim Sweeney was that he had not produced his dog license at the station as requested. Miklan was determined that the law would be obeyed. According to his mother, Jim had been away on the two occasions when the garda officer came calling to the house about the dog license.

As far as Miklan was concerned an officer of the state and therefore the state was being disrespected. His car partner laughed about it and told him to forget it but Miklan had no such intention. Miklan would be known in Ireland as a thick man. This did not just mean a stupid man but an individual who had what a psychologist would recognise as a cognitively disadvantaged condition with complications which a counsellor would attribute to unresolved emotional conflicts. In plain man's language he was a quite stupid man with a very quick temper who could not control himself. This very emotional individual became dangerous when he reinforced his character defects and job dissatisfaction with alcohol. The condition was further exacerbated by the frequent inflated stories he was being told about his graduating class mates doing very well in the flat rental market in Dublin and one in particular who was making a killing in the, even more lucrative, gambling arcades business. All his colleagues knew the effect such stories had on Miklan so, in classic Irish christian style, they sat back and watched his irritation grow. As Miklan mulled over this news he cursed his bad luck and detested this area with its impoverished people even more.

20 November 1976 was a normal Sunday for Gardai 'Miklan' McGrath and Moriarty. They were not looking forward to the boredom of the night shift and occasionally Miklan would drink a pint or two and a few chasers before donning his uniform and going on Sunday night duty. Such behaviour would be frowned upon by his superiors but who would know. Nothing ever happened on the Sunday night shift. His companion, the car driver called Moriarty, did not drink at all on the days he was on duty and would be considered a civil guard in every sense of the word.

2 SERMON

After putting it off until he could do so no longer, Father McCarney was preparing to get down to writing the sermon, the most hated task of the week. He had glanced over St Mark's Gospel for the next day's mass which was Sunday 20 November, the 33rd Sunday in ordinary time. It included the words of warning to be ready because we know neither the day nor the hour. The words of his sermon were taking shape in his mind. He knew this kind of talk filled people with fear and he did not particularly like to use it or dwell on it but today it was unavoidable. He knew that the gospel text referred to the disciples' expectation that the return of Jesus, and therefore the end of the world, was imminent but what harm in turning it around to make people fear their own death because for sure one does not generally know the day or the hour of that event.

 It was there in the gospel and he had also decided to work in a bit of a warning about getting involved in political violence to free Ireland because of the most recent shootings throughout the six counties and further bomb deaths just across the border. Usually he didn't make any mention of such events but he could hardly avoid it today because of the horror of another policeman blown to bits in a neighbouring village. Most unpleasant and maybe some of his parishioners involved – maybe. He knew the people who were involved were unlikely to be in the church but his words might save some other young boys, and girls too, from getting carried away into armed violence with the romantic vision of a united Ireland when they came of age.

This Sunday was also the feast day of St Lawrence O'Toole, archbishop of Dublin, who died around 1180. This information was available in the national diocesan bulletin which carried such items every week. Lawrence was a saint of the church who was a graduate of Glendalough Monastery and had successfully negotiated the political turmoil of his day which included dealing with Henry the second of England.

Like Lawrence, Fr McCarney admired and aspired to the monastic lifestyle because he saw it as the only way of rising above the misery and tedium of the mental state induced by everyday existence. He thought this was the case for all people even those with an exciting and prosperous life or maybe especially for them.

Like Fr McCarney, Lawrence knew the Irish of his day. He saw how treacherous and disloyal they were to each other and on his deathbed in France he expressed his sorrow and horror at what he foresaw for his own people. 'Alas, you poor, foolish people, what will you do now? Who will take care of you in your trouble? Who will help you?' His sorrow would have been much greater had he fully realised the horrors that awaited Ireland and its people in the centuries following his death.

Since his ordination in Maynooth in 1965 Fr McCarney had seen many changes that he did not particularly like but, as a humble curate, had to accept. The bishop ruled the Episcopal roost and people, including the clergy, obeyed. In many ways the priest was more browbeaten by the church and its rules than the civilian flock, even the women. However nothing to be done because he had taken a vow of obedience which he often found difficult. It was a very handy vow if you want to run an army or a church. Blind obedience to Rome was the rule.

 He now said mass facing the congregation and in English. He had always liked the Latin mass but that had all been swept away by the, US lead, modernisation following the 2nd Vatican Council which had been called by Cardinal Roncalli better known as Pope John 23rd. The biggest change and the one that had affected him most was the sermon. He now had not only to live the word of God but also had to preach it. It was compulsory. So it came to pass that every weekend priests up and down the country, himself included, had to sit and write out a sermon on stuff they did not even believe let alone find interesting. He hated it, he hated preaching. Why not let the people make up their own minds. But of course the bishoprical incumbents knew where that would end up. If people were free to think without direction they might lose their religion altogether. He well knew that most had little real religion anyway but week after week he stood up and preached for fifteen minutes as the congregation sat before him in various states of alertness. Among them was Jim Sweeney who had the need to go to mass so that his mother would not be worrying that his soul might be lost for all eternity. Fr McCarney knew there were many Jims in the congregation before him every Sunday.

For a period he had tried to get away with a very, very short sermon. Be good to each other or do unto others as you would have them do to you or even more adventurous stuff like be careful of what you say about your neighbours or even more pointed the one about storing up riches in heaven and not on earth. The bishop heard about his brief oratorical offerings and the parish priest had nudged him towards writing a longer sermon.

Fr McCarney leaned back in his arm chair and, extending the footrest, lay back with his eyes closed in contemplation. Did he himself believe in God at all or prayer or all that stuff that was being broadcast weekly from every pulpit in Ireland? Theology never interested him very much anyway because it was all baloney if there was no God and as for prayers - he saw them as distractions in the mind and who invented religion anyway? It was all man-made. He could never let these things reach the light of day and he had often thought of leaving the church but there was his mother to consider. He was now thirty five and he knew he would have to decide soon because the window of opportunity for setting up home with a woman and children was closing.

He had read Nietzsche and other atheists as well as the saints of his own church. The atheist and theist the world over seemed to be saying the same thing as far as he saw. According to Nietzsche, it is his stomach that mostly reminds man he is not a God. If his confessional experience was any indicator Fr McCarney often thought the Irishman would also need to add onanism to that. According to Nietzsche man must be overcome and each person must choose his own method of overcoming. How he had tried to get that notion across to his parishioners with their pathetic litanies, rosaries and devotions. He often wondered what they were thinking about as they closed their eyes in contemplative prayer. He only knew what he would be thinking about. How could you think about God with a limited human mind? You might as well try thinking about infinity. He knew it was time to reign in them unruly thoughts.

Eddy Murray

He saw fasting as a useful method of overcoming and moving the mind from the low considerations of life like success, money, sex, alcohol and on to higher things, higher feelings, and a higher state of being. All else was hell, but he was becoming convinced that organised religious practice could itself be a block to the higher self. Giving people life recipes to follow was the real road to perdition. Each had to choose his own path. He knew that he had to fast for twenty four hours at least once a week or else he would find himself sinking into the maelstrom of everyday life and circumstance. If he didn't fast he would get depressed, confused and overwhelmed by all that he saw around him never mind all he heard in confession. He opened his eyes and realised the amazingly tortuous headlock he was in and started on his sermon.

'We live in a world which we cannot predict. All of this can be frightening and in the gospel today (Luke 21.5-19) Jesus speaks about it. From his words we may think how little the world has changed in 2000 years. There would be wars and many rumours about wars. There will be persecution of the Church. The words of Jesus reassure us about such happenings which can so disturb us.

Now, unlike the apostles, we know that the end of the world is not about to happen any time soon. Indeed there are some terrible events in our world. Certainly, we need to pause and take stock but life goes on and has to go on. Those who follow God do not take refuge in talk about the end of the world but always seek a way forward, a way to help others. On a personal level we need to be prepared because of the thief in the night'

There he had done it; he had thrown in the favourite terror weapon. Remind them of their death and always be prepared by living a good life, whatever that was.

He knew he still had two more hand written pages to fill, maybe with some anecdote or interesting observation to fill the time, he hated preaching all over again, he hated - no he detested writing sermons. He enjoyed all the other priestly activities, the births, deaths and marriages were fine – but not this.

His mind wandered as he reflected on the simple faith of the people; well to be honest, it was mostly the women who had the faith. Yes indeed it was the women because the men were just there in the chapel because of the women. Those impotent yet powerful mothers and wives who could be relied upon to plant the seed of faith in the home and keep the children safe for eternity. So on it went in a perfect, self perpetuating circle of religion where nobody actually knew what they believed in apart from the mumbled jumbo in the creed. It was a part of the Irish culture that you were born into and if you were lucky or unlucky enough to have a vocation to the priesthood then you got the chance to stand up on the altar every Sunday and speak about it. There were never moments without doubts but these were soon forgotten. He had again caught himself lapsing into his usual distractions, any escape from the horror of the sermon.

'Back to it –all right the thief in the night, tell them again.'

Ok. A cup of tea then get this thing wrapped up. 'We must be watchful because we know not the day nor the hour – neither do the angels in heaven, nor the son but only the father'

'That should do it – nobody knows except the big fella.'

A voice from the kitchen announced that his dinner was ready. Mrs Sweeney came in to cook his dinner every day except Sunday and his designated fast day which varied every week. Usually on Sundays he dined out at the local restaurant or more often at his parents' house. He liked that because they were getting old and he enjoyed their company now more than he had ever done. He was becoming more tolerant of their ways and he had forgiven his mother for inducing his vocation and making his early life a private hell. In reality his vocation was more of a social induction with a drift towards the church which he did nothing to stop until it was too late. A priest in the family was a great blessing. So what, this life was as good as any other but his thoughts drifted back to thinking about living with a woman. Such thought was soon buried under a blanket of events or personal guilt as usual. He always felt the Irish did a good line in guilt, the other national addiction so subtle and imperceptible like tea drinking.

He walked through to the kitchen for his dinner. Mrs Sweeney was preparing to leave. "Just put your dishes in the sink and I will deal with them on

Monday"– were her parting words, then, "See you father"

Very respectful of the priest was Mrs Sweeney. In many ways she was a typical Irish woman.

'Well, not exactly,' mused Fr McCarney.

He had picked up some tittle tattle since his arrival in the parish four years earlier, how she had reared five children on her own but all had left home now. All her sons in England except for Jim, the youngest and she had a daughter, Marilyn, married in a neighbouring parish. Jim had been sent to secondary school to be given a chance at education but was now back living on the family farm. Not exactly a major success story. He knew the mother, like many the one in Ireland, had harboured notions of the priesthood for Jim or maybe he'd be a doctor or solicitor. Instead he got thrown out of college in his second year for some sort of insubordination. All that wasted money and he was now hanging about on the small farm this past five years or so. Someone had to run the place and make a few pound since the father was not around. Things happen for a purpose or what's necessary creates the purpose. There was also a daughter in America who never came home and was rarely mentioned.

He ate his dinner in silence and pondered what else he would write to finish his sermon as he recalled the end of the gospel – 'Heaven and earth will pass away, but my words will not pass away. When its branch becomes tender and sprouts leaves, you know that summer is near. In the same way when you see these things happening, know that he is near. Amen, I say to you, this generation will not pass away until all these things have taken place.'

He liked that bit about the trees growing and knew the people would too so he wondered how he could work it in to the end of his sermon – a soft ending with a bit of hope rather than the 'day nor the hour' terror.

He put the sermon out of his mind and resumed his favourite position. Sitting in his recliner with his feet up, head back, eyes shut and listening to music. Chopin's piano music was coming out of the radio. He drifted with the minute waltz and felt happy immersed in its playful rhythms. He thought Chopin certainly knew how to write music for the piano.

He was tired after his enforced intellectual exertions and slipped into an after dinner nap.

3 SUNDAYS

Sundays in the Sweeney household had remained unchanged over the years. This was the day of enforced rest because non-essential, servile work was frowned upon by the church and besides, the neighbours would talk. The walk to the chapel and Sunday Mass was the primary activity of the day followed by the purchase of the Sunday Press or Independent which was sold from the back of the newsagent's car at the chapel gate. The paper bought depended on your family position on the civil war of 1922. The Republican Fianna Failer bought the Sunday Press while the Fine Gael Freestater bought the Independent. The newspaper used to be sold before mass but some of the free spirits would sit on the kneeling board of the back pew reading the paper during mass so the practice was stopped.

Around eleven o'clock, and back from mass, Jim settled down at the end of the kitchen table to his paper and a light breakfast of sweetened tea, multiple slices of heavily buttered toast and homemade marmalade. He always made the mistake of eating too much toast so that when the dinner was ready he wasn't properly hungry but he still managed to eat the most of it. The mother took one slice of toast with her tea.

The Sunday Press was the only newspaper coming into the house all week and Jim always started with the sports pages. Donegal had been coming up in the GAA in recent years because the improved economic prospects in the county meant that less of the youth had to emigrate and so club football was going strong as was the county team. Nevertheless he had doubtful hopes or hopeful doubts that they would ever win an Ulster title never mind the all Ireland. He had no real interest in the club football scene in Britain but occasionally glanced at Manchester United's performance. This was a legacy of the time he had spent over there on the building sites and in the canning factories where football occupied a good deal of the lunch time chats. He did know that United had beaten Liverpool 2-1 in the last FA cup but were still in the, post Busby, period of decline with the heydays of the Best and Charlton era long behind them.

The political unrest in the North had a beneficial outcome for the regions on both sides of the border because Britain was pouring money into job creation schemes in the communities in the six counties. This was a futile attempt to create employment aimed at weaning the people off their support for the IRA. It was inevitable that some of the money sloshing about splashed across the border in the form of 'cash in hand' jobs and support for various enterprises.

An example of this British generosity took the form of, loosely controlled, EEC subsidies and grants for farmers. The loose control was government policy because a farmer with a few pounds in his pocket would be thought less likely to support the IRA.

A typical development was the construction of concrete lanes through farms, up mountains and down glens. Every farm in the northern border region got a long concrete farm lane if needed or not, usually not. The contractor could make money fast by cutting back on the concrete in the lane. As long as the edges showed six inches of concrete it didn't really matter to the department official that the centre was filled with gravel and a thin covering of concrete. Another favourite was the sheep vacation scheme. Subsidies were paid on the number of sheep owned so it was a fairly simple matter to arrange for the same flock to be counted several times on both sides of the border because sheep, unlike cattle, had no individual identifiers. Jim never fully participated in these handy money schemes, not because of any real moral objections but probably due to a failure of nerve or lack of connections with the other participating farmers.

Occasionally he might think he had made some headway in being in touch with the local farming community. At the mart or some social event he might come across two neighbours in their flat caps and boots in a discussion about matters agricultural or more likely exchanging tittle tattle which goes under the general name of gossip. They would say hello but if he approached with some valid question to break the ice, he was always met with the same reception. The question would be answered alright by one of them but that was it. The end of the discussion with him was made clear, the shutters were down. They could not and would not resume their free flowing conversation until he had moved on. He had interrupted their discourse. So once again he felt outside of things and he would shuffle off as usual in a state of internal embarrassment vowing never to make any such attempt again. This had happened more than once and he always got caught. If only he could maintain his resolve never to make an approach to them again. Who needed the bastards anyway? Still, he reasoned, he would be better with some communication with his neighbours but how to achieve what seemed to come so naturally and easily to everyone else. Was it like this everywhere for him he wondered? At moments like that he knew he needed to get away, he had to escape. To where?

One incident of this was still fresh in his mind. The previous Saturday he had been standing at the bar with just a few customers present. Sitting beside him was one of the local cattle dealers called Martin McVerry. Martin was considered a man of substance; looked up to in the area, married to a primary school teacher and given to wearing tweed whenever not in his cattle jobbing uniform which included trousers rolled up to the top of his orange boots with their grass green cow dung stains. His ability, or that of his henchmen, to judge cattle would be much better than that of the average small farmer who he would always get the better of in any deal and not be slow to talk about it.

Jim ventured his usual style of icebreaker question. "Are cattle making a good price this year Martin?"

The dealer squinted out from under the peak of his flat cap with a half grin on his face and paused for a good while before offering the question to two local men who were beside him at the bar.

"Boys, are cattle making a good price this year?"

Jim knew immediately he had once again become an object of derision and wounded, he retreated into his own silent contemplation.

Most border regions also have a vibrant smuggling economy where the more entrepreneurial spirits of the area enrich themselves by transferring goods across the frontier without paying the excise duty. In earlier times especially

Eddy Murray

in the war years and later forties and fifties it used to be dry goods like cigarettes, whiskey or butter that crisscrossed the Irish border but smuggling such items had become generally unprofitable by the seventies due to tax harmonisation measures associated with EEC membership.

Therefore smuggling had largely moved on from the traditional cross border transfer and disposal of goods to more lucrative and creative activities. This might involve an imaginative interpretation of European export regulations. Typically, a lorry load of pigs or other commodity such as wheat travelling from N. Ireland to the Republic might attract an export subsidy or vice versa. It was a simple matter of driving through the official customs post to receive the necessary export stamp on the documentation followed by a short return trip to the country of departure by an unapproved road without customs. The same pigs might have crossed the border several times and collected several subsidies before finally making it to slaughter.

Compliant customs men on the UK side of the border were always useful. One such was an Englishman called Max Hull who made the mistake of taking a four-week long summer holiday to visit his sister in Birmingham. Max was a queer which was the normal designation at the time before the curious use of the word gay was adopted to describe the individual so directed. He was accepted as useful in the area and would stand untroubled at the local bar with his curved, womanly hips filling his light blue jeans. An Englishman would have been considered to be a more rigid enforcement officer than any local variation, especially the Catholic who was always thought to be up to something. Of course this had no basis in reality because the Catholic in a civil service job like the customs would be very diligent indeed in the service of his master. Upon his return from Brum his superiors called Max in and asked him to explain the fact that detection of illicit cross-border movements had increased considerably in his absence. He explained this by pointing out that the export-import agents had obviously tried to take advantage of his absence but fortunately had not succeeded due to the diligence of his replacement colleague.

Clearly the British army policy of cratering unapproved roads at the border interfered with this trade but ways were found to overcome such local difficulties. For example one enterprising fellow built a long shed which straddled the border so it was a simple matter of letting the exported pigs walk through the shed to arrive back for reshipment. The authorities always took a period of time, usually months or years, to enact measures which neutralised such activities by which time the traders had moved on to their next business with a suitable export loophole. Jim did get some irregular cash flow by facilitating this export-import business but it was likely that much of the dividend went to the IRA.

Things were starting to look up financially for Jim of late. He had been offered the opportunity of using his farmyard as an overnight lorry park and fuel storage depot for the newly emerging diesel smuggling trade. However, he never got directly involved in the cross border action mainly because he could not drive the tankers and heavy lorries used.

His mother's voice, as she peeled the last of the pink potatoes which she was dropping into a pot of water, slightly interrupted his reading.

"When you are finished with that would you bring in a few sticks for the fire, it's getting low."

Jim did not even look up or reply which prompted his mother to make a larger splash with her next potato – "did you hear me?" This caused a momentary lapse from his paper and a vacant answer, "In a minute, I heard you."

"You could reply."

This was the usual extent of the conversation between the pair and it did not indicate animosity but a rather agreeable and relaxed familiarity. It would take some major news to cause any variation in this level of verbal communication between them and even then very few words would be exchanged.

When he had read the sports sections there was little else of interest for Jim in the paper apart from a glance over the front page news which was often to do with the latest atrocity of the troubles in the six counties. When finished with the paper he would fold it in quarter and place it on his mother's armchair where it would sit until she had finished making the dinner. Before the week was out he knew she would have read it all apart from the sports pages.

Jim got out of his chair, placed the folded newspaper on the armchair and was making his way out the kitchen door towards the stick shed.

"Ash" Was the one word he heard from his mother as he was leaving the kitchen. He knew that seasoned ash was the best burner and heat producer which would be needed to make sure the dinner was ready by one o'clock.

The dinner of roast chicken from their own flock was served without ceremony apart from the grace before meals given out by the mother to a muttered rendition by Jim who blessed himself when he thought it was finished. Mashed potatoes, cabbage from the garden and gravy with onions. That was another thing Jim did not particularly like. Strangling chickens with their yellow feet trussed up and hanging from a nail in the byre. They always obligingly held their head back and he would catch it between his first and second finger. That warm feeling of the head followed by a small downward pressure and then the sickening sinew wrenching, disjointing and elongation of the neck followed by the frantic, final flapping.

After dinner the remains of the chicken were covered with a tea cloth and removed from the heat of the kitchen to the scullery which was always cooler, winter or summer. Food for the dog was made up from the scraps left over from the dinner including chicken bones. Jim had heard that chicken bones should not be given to a dog but his Rover seemed to have had no difficulty over the years with them and indeed seemed to relish them. The dog only got tinned food at Christmas or when visitors from England brought some in as a canine treat.

The final dinner related activity was to take the boiled potato peelings from the fire, mix them with a handful or two of layers mash before taking the warm mixture out to the hens that always came running when he appeared with or without feeding for them. He imagined that warm food would be good for them on a cold day like today.

When he had fed the chickens he entered an outhouse and put on his parka overcoat and wellingtons. He buttoned up the coat as he emerged from the door of the shed into the cold of the yard whistling for the dog that dashed from his own shed where he slept on a bed of hay. With the dog running alongside he set off on his usual Sunday walk over the land to fodder the cattle and note any jobs he might need to do before the winter was out. He was fully aware that making a note of a job was no guarantee that it would be done this winter or any winter until it became absolutely necessary. The dog was always his close companion on these journeys and he had him trained to come to heel with a whistle if required. Most of the time he let the dog run free which seemed to be exactly what he enjoyed best.

One job for noting was fencing which was a permanent item for attention that was not usually seen to until the cattle had broke out several times onto the road or into the neighbour's land. Both events were a cause for concern because one neighbour, a first cousin of his own, with whom he was historically engaged in an unexplained cold war, would simply drive the wandering cattle to the road and that had potentially lethal consequences. Despite this danger, the minimum amount of fencing was carried out. He often bought posts, barbed wire and steeples with firm intentions to make a good fence between his land and his neighbours but he usually never got round to it. Another neighbouring man, Mr O'Donlon, lived on the other side of him. His mother was Scottish and he considered himself a cut above the locals. He would occasionally see Jim's posts as he drove or walked past and would never miss an opportunity to borrow a few of 'them posts'. This man was a practising alcoholic.

For some reason Jim never said no to this request and the borrowed posts soon became part of a long term and then forgotten loan. For a time after the borrowing Jim would determine in his mind that he would ask for the posts back but somehow never got round to it. Well, Jim reasoned yet again, maybe it was just as well not to fall out with all the neighbours because you never know when you might need their help with a sick or hard calving cow. Still he thought what a bind he was in where he was afraid to ask for his own property back in case he fell out with a neighbour.

Such thoughts filled his mind for a brief consideration before dismissal and reversion to more immediate matters. The pub tonight and the visit to the dance hall entered his thoughts before he was distracted by the dog running alongside him. Rover was busy making energetic sorties with his nose twitching along the scent of last night's animal trails or attempting the more adventurous pursuit of a low flying bird which he had no chance of catching.

The low November sun was already bright orange and dipping towards the rim of the mountain as he arrived at the cattle that advanced towards him, in expectation of feeding, when he entered the field. The dog went into full sheepdog stalking mode, lying low to the ground as the cattle approached. Jim had never trained him but he seemed to have an instinctive ability to herd animals and be generally useful for driving and gathering cattle or sheep. Jim had to be careful if the cows had young calves with them because they would often attack any dog or person in those circumstances.

He removed two bales of hay from the covered stack, fenced off in the corner of the field. He carried them across to a dry bank and cut the twine using his Swiss army knife which had been given to him by his father many years before. He opened the bales on the dry bank under the shelter of a spreading ash tree and divided the hay around so that each of the thirteen beasts could feast without jostling each other. The hay was good quality and the sweet smell reminded him of the hot summer weather they had in June and July past. The setting sun was shining and warm so he sat on a stone in the shelter of the tree with his back resting against its broad trunk and, shading his eyes from the red glow with his two hands, he watched his cattle enjoying the hay for a while. He thought he might get one of them peaked flat caps. He was trying to figure out which of the weanling, nine month old, calves would fetch the best price. The land in the area was poor and could not fatten cattle which were sold at mart for transfer to farmers on the better fattening land of the midland counties like Longford or Westmeath or even further south.

He glanced over at the fairy fort which was nothing more than a group of trees on a little hillock about fifty yards from where he sat. Whatever about fairy superstition nonsense it is a fact that no one would risk taking anything from the fairies so the trees were never touched or cut down for timber. Bad luck would fall on anyone contravening this fairy regulation. No one did.

Jim was not a good judge of cattle because this is an art which is passed from father to son with lessons beginning in childhood. Jim's father never lived at home for any prolonged period and in any case it was likely that his own cattle judging skills might have been defective too. He had been pleasantly surprised once at the mart when, what he thought was, a scrawny looking heifer made a good price. The auctioneer had introduced the calf in very favourable terms.

" Boys, what will you offer me for this fine growthy girl."

Jim was pleased by the feeling of standing there beside the auctioneer as bidding took the price up to £685. This was a superb price for a young heifer which usually sold for less than the bullocks, because of their lower beef content, unless they were showing potential as breeders. This was a rare event and usually he would step down from the stand having shamed and dishonoured his name by accepting a lowish price for his beasts. This was one of the reasons he hated the mart because his only alternative was to take his stock back home and show them again in another mart the next week with no guarantee of improvement. It cost three pounds to take each animal back home and another three to return it a week later.

A good price for a male nine month old bullock would be £550. Including EEC subsidies, his ten cows would produce an annual income of about seven thousand pounds in a good year. Out of this he had to pay all expenses such as extra feeding or hay bought in and general harvesting and farm maintenance costs which left him about £4000 clear. Small money indeed compared to work in a factory or on a building site. He could usually supplement this farm income with the dole of about one hundred pounds per week so his total income was about nine thousand pounds per annum excluding any extras.

The other reason for his hatred of the winter mart was the smelly, draughty coldness and brutality of the place. His calves were always born around Christmas or January to be ready for the November livestock sales after a summer's feeding on green grass. The peasant farmers always came late to the mart with their cattle so that they would not be first up and consequently these small rural sales always started late with a finish after dark. While he waited for the auction to start he would be surprised to see a neighbour, called Frank Cullen, in amongst the beasts in the cattle pens, with a metal comb grooming and fluffing up the hair on his own beasts. Jim wondered if this would make any real difference in the ring but still admired his obvious pride in his animals and wondered why he himself was not similarly moved.

Jim was usually early in the mart and was often one of the first to face the hammer ordeal and this did not help the price he got because the bidding had not got going properly. However it did mean he would avoid the drama associated with loading cattle in the dark. Trying to gather up and load cattle in a small rural mart in the dark is a rare experience which Jim imagined should be on any Irish culture or tourist trail, filled as it is with much animal beating and roaring from agitated man and beast. Every mart contained a good percentage of weanlings which were strongish calves just separated from their mothers. These animals roared continuously in obvious distress especially when the man with the stick drove them into, out of and round the ring with a fairly elevated degree of beating to ensure beastly compliance. The stick might casually strike the rump or nose depending on the requirements of the drover and Jim did not like to see such treatment of his own young animals. Still, he reasoned, steaks had to get to the plates of the people.

He finished his market musings and hoped the weather would stay dry so the ground would firm up after the heavy rain of the previous week. If the ground stayed wet he would have to bring the cattle into the byre and this involved a lot of extra work. Many farmers had built slatted sheds for over-wintering their cattle but Jim had not yet taken up the EEC grants on offer for this purpose. He thought he might do it in the spring and then he thought he might not because he was undecided about whether he wanted to stay on looking after the small, thirty two acre, farm. It would all depend on how the diesel trade worked out.

He did not really enjoy the work and he especially did not like having to do jobs like dosing the cattle which had to be completed twice a year, then there were the two government tests for brucellosis and tuberculosis. But there was always his mother to consider, and then dealing with sick beasts or even dead ones, then the careful watching of the cows for signs of agitation and homo-erotic behaviour which would indicate they were in heat so he could call the artificial inseminator. If the fertile period was missed he would have to watch all over again the next month or lose that cow's calf and income. He would talk about it with his brothers when they came home for Christmas.

It was getting dark as he approached the farm house. He knew his mother would be dozing in the armchair with the newspaper fallen on the ground beside her. He knew her life had been hard enough but she never complained and from time to time he had warm feelings towards her. She woke from her light sleep when he entered the kitchen. He sat down on his usual chair at the end of the table saying, "I might take those three remaining calves to the mart next week. It will save having to buy hay and the price was right good last week according to yer man." Indicating with his thumb towards the house of the borrowing, alcoholic neighbour. His mother knew he did not really like the farming life.

He boiled the kettle and made a cup of tea which he drank with a piece of homemade bread and blackcurrant jam and butter. His mother just took a cup of tea. Jim felt a bit sleepy himself and he lay down on the sofa at the other side of the fire to his mother.

He woke to the sound of an Irish reel on the radio and it lifted his spirits as such music usually did. He always enjoyed ceili music on the radio and his favourite programme was ceili house requests that went out weekly on Radio Eireann. He listened to it with his mother every Saturday night. He loved happy Irish music but unfortunately he found a lot of it sad and dreary.

He looked out the window at the dark evening and announced he was in two minds about going out to the pub at all. The problem was he would have to walk there and probably back and he was wondering if it was worth the trouble. His mother always hoped he would stay in the house especially on a winter's night but she knew he had to go out from time to time and she also knew he would jump up shortly, pull on his coat and simply say – 'see you later'. Later meant the following morning because he never got back before midnight and if he went to the dance hall it could be one or two in the morning before he arrived home.

Shortly after the Irish music programme on the radio ended, he jumped up, put on his coat saying "See you later" as he left the house and pulled the door behind him.

Rover had to be closed in the shed before he left or he would have been with him to the pub. His final act before departure was to close the chicken house. He remembered the last time he forgot to do this and a wild mink had got in and savaged every bird. That kind of event leaves a bad feeling that lasts for several weeks. A kind of feeling of bad luck on the place.

He glanced up at the starry night sky sparkling above him as he closed the farmyard gate and made his way onto the road.

Eddy Murray

4 HOMEWARD

Jim had decided to walk home from the pub that Sunday night without calling into the ballroom for three reasons. He allowed two of these into his conscious consideration but he still found difficulty admitting the third which was more complex.

The first allowed reasons was that the band playing was called Swarbriggs Plus 2 who had been Ireland's entry to the Eurovision song contest and the place would be full of young people dressed up in widely flared trousers and jeans. The second reason was that the entrance fee had been increased to £2 from the usual £1. Besides the music would be pop with very little chance of a waltz. Shaking was out of the question because he felt daft. Jim had always liked to have the security of a grip on his dance partner with the old time or slow waltz his favourite.

In any case that was all in the past because of late he found that all he would do was gaze through drink dimmed eyes across the dance floor from the middle of the standing throng of men. This was the diminishing band of losers like himself who had missed the boat to romance or at least marriage and a family. There was no comfort to be gained from being a member of that group of ever hopeful wretches. There they were peering across the dance floor as the rush for the women began at the start of each set. This was the kernel of the third and disallowed reason for his passing the dance hall and walking on home; this was the inescapable, uncomfortable, terror laden reality which he had difficulty with.

The boat had sailed without him and many times he regretted his failure to follow up on a definite offer of love from Gabrielle who simply said to him when he tried to approach her again, 'You had your chance'. The words still echoed through his burned out consciousness when he remembered how

Eddy Murray

he had been lying there on the ground in the darkness beside her, after the dance, moving his fingers through the delicious, lubricious softness between her legs. He still could not figure out why he pulled back when she weakly resisted and said that it would be wrong to remove them..... He realised later the same evening, with bitter regret, now magnified many times since, that this was simply an invitation to do just that. Yes, he regretted that lost opportunity a year earlier which was still still clear in his memory and repeated to excite himself many times since.

Or the two young protestant girls even earlier when he was about seventeen and encountered them sitting on a stone ditch one summer's day at the village festival. Again the words and face of one of them came back to him even now. Chewing gum and sitting with the black school uniform dress riding high on her thigh she said, 'What's the lightest thing in the world? Then noticing no answer replied quickly 'a thought will lift it' as she chewed her gum. A Temptress of the Holy Ghost indeed and still he didn't take up the offer. Put it down to inexperience and youth on that occasion.

So he now felt embarrassed going into the mating place and he felt ill at ease there, fish out of water, odd man out, object of derision and so on in the inescapable, self inflicted, terminology of the social outcast.

He walked on home thinking about the scene in the dance hall. The sweaty swarm of mini-skirted women dancing and having fun with each other or with their male partners. He had been a silent, semi-desperate observer of that scene for the past few years since he turned 25. He had always felt older or maybe odder than the usual dance goer even when he wasn't but now with every passing year it was getting closer to reality.

He wanted a woman and dreamed of children but he codded himself that he would wait until his mother had passed away. He was fully aware that she was still going strong and, in any case, he rarely let these notions rise to the point which would demand action. If he did, he might gain some insight into his predicament and do something about it because there were still matchmakers in the country. This method of arranging a partner was considered somehow shameful and second rate. So on he walked through the shadows cast by the dim crossroad lights, past the packed car park and soon the dance hall music had faded too. No cars on the road so he had no chance of a lift home. It was Sunday night and anyone drinking was not driving because of the garda presence in the area.

He walked on into the dark night and pondered on some of his more generalised dance hall memories. The crush and rush that would carry him on a sea of struggling male bodies towards the lines of women waiting to be asked when the music started. The body of men would advance as one heaving mass towards the women across the floor. The first rush saw many successfully select a partner while others, Jim usually included, were carried by the wave of male bodies along the female throng towards the end of the line at the bottom of the hall. He would make the odd futile and hopeless gesture   or spoken word to the occasional woman but usually his outstretched hand and gazing eye failed to connect and he was carried on past to emerge at the bottom of the hall with his body intact but mind damaged once more. Then he might consider doing it all again and join the second rush which by now had thinned out considerably. The result was always the same of late. However he did remember similar experiences when he was much younger and he had reasoned then that all would be different when he went to university where he would meet women socially. As it turned out it was not different at all.

So, thoroughly exposed as a first and second time failure he felt he had no chance so he would slink back to the comfort of the side wall among the other men who had also failed or not even tried to secure a dance and wondering who had seen him. Glad he had escaped until the next time. He repeated this a few times then usually gave up and went home. So for several years now he never really enjoyed the dance hall and went there more in hope than with any expectation that he would succeed in acquiring a woman. Was he too small, too wide, too red haired, too old fashioned in dress, too poor, maybe he didn't look the woman in the eye; maybe the smell of alcohol but everyone drank before going in to Irish dance halls nowadays. When he was younger he would have considered it totally improper to ask a woman to dance if you smelt of alcohol but now he was well practised and never thought about it. His submerged thinking rarely rose above the smoulder and there it remained in a steamy stew of fenced off confusion that he kept adding to every week. Alcohol was now his support and refuge.

Jim's mind moved to the public house encounters earlier. He never really enjoyed the pub either but seemed destined to attend regularly because – because it was there and presenting himself twice every weekend seemed like inescapable reality. After the first pint or two the pain was dulled. For the first mile of his homeward journey he continued to mull over the evening's events and people. In particular he felt unease about meeting Jimmy Redmond, a man of about 55 who always mentioned 'I know your mammy' Yes, Jim thought, of course he knew her because everyone knew everyone in this rural community so why was this man repeating this phrase. 'I know your mammy, or was that I knew your mammy?' It did not matter because it had the same meaning. This peasant was saying something different because he kept repeating it every time he encountered him in the pub.

Jim never did allow himself to examine the repeated phrase 'I know your Mammy' being uttered in a pub which was itself not done. Mentioning the name of a woman, especially your mother, in a pub in Ireland was, somehow, considered socially unacceptable and disrespectful in any context. Never until this evening was he prepared in his mind to countenance the facts instead of hurriedly, ashamedly suppressing them from his mind. His usual method of dealing with such comments was to let them fester and bubble in the lower reaches but never allow them to rise to the level of consciousness where they could be examined and neutralised. Today, tonight he would exorcise this demon. Tonight he was determined.

This evening would be different. Years earlier he had learned from his long absent and now deceased father that his mother had been pregnant before he married her. If this was the case then it is possible that Redmond had indeed –'known his mother'. He would not allow the action to be called making love because of the individual involved who was as typical a peasant Irish man as you could meet. Filled with low cunning and little of the spiritual intelligence that elevates the human being above the beast. Though Jim wondered, within his limited experience, if it was not a fanciful notion that any human could ever rise above the level of the beast in the final analysis.

If the likes of that grinning, spavined fellow ever got to 'know' a woman he would consider that as a victory and hold over her, a power even if the act occurred only once or maybe never except in his idiot mind. He had 'known' her and need not bother himself with her again. If she was not known as a real easy mark then she could be used to enhance himself by making his drunken, bawdy innuendo in the pub. Such was Irish peasant life and indeed the same pattern is often found in primitive and not so primitive peoples the world over. In the mating game the female must resist the advances of the male or forever carry the mark of shame. In Irish society this mark is transferred by the casual insult in the pub or shouts on the street. In less advanced societies such females may receive a physical mark or scar on the face or worse. It had always puzzled Jim why this was the case and he had not worked out a reason except to think of it as a relic of primeval and savage forces where wild beasts marked out their territory and secured their females by violence.

But if it had occurred, if that fellow had 'known' the woman who was now his mother then the sly insinuation in the 'I know your mammy' was as destructive and humiliating as it was intended to be. A woman who was known by several men in the area would not be held in very high esteem for sure and forever. This would also place her children at the bottom of the local social order... white trash. The folk memory of the Irish man with his penchant for exaggeration and transfer of information down the generations by the spoken word would ensure that the story would be told forever. Not in any long winded manner but instead it would be transmitted and arrive to the listener in an abbreviated and spiked comment. He knew from experience that the lonely and ill people who make up the Irish bar clientele are well skilled in these arts. This fellow who 'knew' his mother was simply confirming what he had always known about them.

So it went on as he repeated his discussion with himself and how he might find a solution. If he had been a Sicilian he knew exactly what he would have to do.

There at last he had allowed it into his conscious mind for the first time and the only result was a general feeling of disgust at the minds of the peasant Irish especially where sex was concerned. He felt no anger towards his mother but was now more fully aware why she really did not want him drinking in the pub and meeting the 'likes' of people like that. Jim knew now that his mother was fully aware of the attitude that such low down male mongrels would have towards her. Yet he knew she could have gone to England as his father had often suggested on one of his home visits. Jim admired the fact that she had decided to stand her ground and turn to Jesus as her strength and support in the face of the Catholic Church itself, Irish male society and of course its supine womenfolk. Yet was this not just another trap? Had she not made a pact with the devil and entered a prison of the mind built by the very church responsible for the thinking of people like Redmond.

So what to do? There was no chance of discussing it with the woman who had turned to God and religion as her only bulwark against the ugly, rapacious and despising attention of men in the area. No chance of that at all but it did not stop further impossible conversations taking shape in his own mind as imagined with his mother - 'Did you? Well did you? With Jimmy Redmond? Was it a one off or a regular event? Were there any others? Did you not realise the way that our society is and how it deals with offenders?'

It all fitted into place now – it all made more sense – why the neighbours never called at the house, why the cowardly refusal to supply milk to the young mother alone with her young children that he had heard his mother talking about at very rare, darker moments in her life. How the priest would have played his part too because in the end it was the desire of the church to keep good moral order in the locality and 'loose' women created the conditions for the direct opposite – so then why did so many women turn to the church to solve the problem created by them in the first place? – The questions kept coming and going round in his head. He knew there were no answers other than - that is how it was - how it is.

He decided he would allow himself a few more yards of this type of circular thinking before he would move on to different things – higher things. He listened to the sound of his own footsteps slapping on the black tar road as he padded his way homeward and also became aware of the river flowing behind the roadside hedge. The rushing water was making occasional noises as it crashed around rocks or splashed over fallen trees on its way east towards the ocean.

That was it! Such natural distractions were more pleasurable and led him into thinking about ways he could achieve a state of mental stability where he experienced peace instead of the constant nagging of jagged thoughts in the background.

He had thought it strange when he heard Fr McCarney say that, the atheist, Nietzsche thought that man was something to be overcome to be risen above which was exactly what Jesus was saying. He thought this was quite a leap to say that the believer in God and the non-believer were saying the same thing. His thoughts lingered a while on this as he entered the second mile of his homeward journey. 'Man is something to be overcome' would be the same as saying that the individual should control his appetites and become a free man. The idea appealed to Jim because he was aware that his life and mind could never be described as free. In fact it was quite the opposite if he ever was honest enough to accept his reality. Fr McCarney always said that fasting was one way of achieving this overcoming but Jim would never link it with prayer or religion. He could never understand what prayer was about at all or religion or churches or sermons. Well he knew such thinking went nowhere but at least it was successfully distracting him from his local, trivial and corrosive horror.

He made his mind up then and there like he had done so many times but this time it would be different. He would achieve his new and elevated mental state so that no small time, malodorous peasant mind could reach him. He would achieve this freedom by fasting and abstinence especially from drinking. He knew he had to be careful that he did not become mistaken for a religious person.

That was it; he could relax for the remainder of his journey home, only one mile to go. He would understand his mother and he would forgive her all the hard living she had imposed on him when he was growing up. The casual abuse of all the children in the family by harsh words and deeds that came so easily to his own mother and to so many Irish parents. He never understood why it happened; was it a legacy of being a member of a doomed and defeated race of people, eternally depressed? The tortured, twisted souls then emerged from these homes to inhabit the world and try to pass themselves off as human. He would understand and forgive it all – tomorrow.

He was interrupted in his high-flown thinking by the sound of a car in the distance behind him. If his luck was in he would maybe get a lift for the last mile home. The thought of home made him hungry and he could already taste the salty chicken sandwich with a glass of milk followed by a cup of sweet tea.

The sound of the car approaching from behind him had become louder. The headlights were soon flashing along the road beside him and lighting up the green ferns and rushes sticking out from the banks alongside. He half turned to face the car to make sure he was not another victim of the Irish motorist and that the driver could recognise him if he was to give him a lift. As the car passed him he noticed the two figures in the front and knew immediately it was the guards. He was relieved when they drove past him and he felt the rush of the cold night air as the car moved past and on up the road.

He resumed his musing on the nature of human freedom and how it could be achieved. On he walked and he could hear the rush of river water as it washed over stones and fallen trees. He walked along a sweeping, bending stretch of the road where the water flowed silently behind a hedged bank. The water noise decreased because, along this stretch of the road, the river entered a deep gulley and flowed silently through clay banks. Silent waters, dark waters and more dangerous waters still because of their quiet depths.

A mile to go to his bed and his mother's shout 'is that you?' she looked after him well but he hated it. He wanted to say every night.

"Who to fuck do you think it is?"

But, resigned to his fate of living with his mother with no wife, no children he always answered patiently.

"Yes it's me."

The fire would be dying in the grate and no kettle boiling but the electric would soon boil him up a cup of tea and he could almost hear his mother's voice.

"Wash your hands."

Every Sunday night the same, "Wash your hands."

 Did she think he got lucky and his hands might be contaminated with the juices of some country girl? Well it had not happened again so in his mind he was again salting a piece of cold cooked chicken to make himself that rough sandwich then quietly drawing the blankets over himself in the cold bed. Like every Sunday night.

His thoughts were interrupted by the diminishing drone of the car as its red rear lights seemed to glow intensely through the bare whitethorn hedge round a slight bend in the road. About 400 yards up the road the car was turning and was moving back towards him. He didn't like the gardai or one in particular called Miklan. He recalled what his mother had told him about that guard calling to the house about the dog license and he remembered her words 'Get that dog license and leave it in at the barracks because we don't want that kind of people calling at the house again'. He did not want the guards near his house either because if they were nosing about they would be sure to spot any smuggling activity.

 The hedges on each side of the road were high so there was no chance of getting off the road. He hoped they would drive on past but he saw they were slowing down and moving at a crawl towards him. Then the roof spotlight was switched on and pointed at him. There was no mistake, they were showing an interest in him.

By good fortune he was beside an entrance to a foot-bridge leading to a neighbouring house. He decided it would be a good time to make a visit to a neighbour so he turned and headed onto the bridge as the car approached with its window rolled down.

5 CAR

Junior Garda Moriarty reversed the squad car out of the car park at Tirmore Garda Station and grimaced over to Sergeant McGrath better known by his nickname Miklan. It was 11.00 pm. Their, ten hour, Sunday evening shift which included two hours overtime had begun 60 minutes earlier and they had spent the last hour writing up reports. Like policemen the world over these gardai hated writing reports.

Moriarty disliked this part of the country but for MIklan it was more a matter of deep and active hatred. He had thought he was well connected in the gardai with a couple of uncles who had long service and were on the point of retirement. He had one uncle at the rank of Inspector and the other a Superintendent. With these relatives in such exalted positions he had expected a key posting around Dublin city, maybe even on the traffic motorcycle section. This was his first choice of career and he had made this known to the selection officer. The motor cycle traffic squad were the sexiest guys on the force with powerful BMW machines and snappy leather gear all supplied by the state. They saw themselves as movie or TV bike types who never failed to don dark glasses in the sun or even out of the sun.

Moriarty spoke; "Let us go into the valley of the shadow of death, let us boldly go into Death Valley once more."

Miklan made no reply as the car headlights picked out the 30 mile limit sign and he tried to tune the radio to North West country. He was a keen country and western fan and the girls all loved his jiving but it only worked if the girl knew how to do it because Miklan had no dancing skills. What the girls really liked was the fact that he was a garda officer with a pensionable job and didn't smell of cow dung on a regular basis. Reception was bad and he cursed the crackling radio; then in rapid sequence he cursed the night, the car, the town, the radio again and the job – "fuck this cunt of a town, fuck this cunt of a radio and fuck this cunt of a car."

When he had exhausted his repertoire of objects to be cursed he rested, out of breath and depleted. The car driver had noted the rising crescendo and intensity of the barrage which got more exorbitant in exclamation as he progressed down the list.

"You not happy then," said his driver and continued, "I told you it was a bad idea to be taking them pints before going on the night shift. You know that drinking is bad for staying awake at night and we have a long night ahead till eight in the morning."

The driver was aware of his colleague's character defects and short temper, especially with alcohol on board and he was careful to keep things jovial. He was also aware that the man was his line manager, his sergeant, who wrote the reports on which his promotion prospects depended.

The two gardai were tasked with patrolling the border region of Tirmore to Ballyleagh to make sure that no 'IRA lads' were getting up to their 'divillment' as Moriarty was accustomed to proclaim to his colleague who was not sure how to take him. Anything suspicious would be investigated but it was a good bet that nothing would happen to relieve the boredom. It was a dark November night but they welcomed the fact that the rain of the previous three weeks had given way to clear skies with a crescent moon and a full set of sparkling stars.

The car drove at a steady 40 mph as it nosed its way through the darkness, past the music of the Dreamland Ballroom and on through the crossroads at Glenlackan before starting the six mile journey to Ballyleagh.

The two uniformed branch men discussed the possibility of doing the rural pubs because it was not unusual to find them full of drinkers long after the legal limit of 10.30 plus 30 minutes drinking up time. It was simply a matter of pulling up outside the premises and listening for sounds of revelry from within. The owner would have made sure all the doors were locked and there were no chinks of light emerging so noise was the only clue that would make entering the premises worthwhile. If gardai entered to find a pub without illegal drinkers then they felt foolish and usually avoided such an outcome.

They decided against it mainly because Miklan smelt of drink himself. So they drove on in the full knowledge that each pub would probably have a full set of illegal drinkers sitting comfortably, possibly with a fiddler or accordionist lifting their spirits, with their pints in the welcoming heat of the turf fire.

About two mile out of the village the car headlights picked out a walking figure on the right hand side of the road, barely visible apart from his white reflective armband but on the correct side for a pedestrian. They drove past until about 400 yards up the road when Miklan suddenly exclaimed, "Isn't that that Jim cunt who was giving me the slip all week, turn round and let us see what he has to say for himself now."

Moriarty looked across at the sergeant and said, "Let it go Miklan, we need to keep going because we have to be in Ballyleagh at twelve or miss the tea break and you need some strong coffee."

Miklan was having none of it and shouted, "Turn to fuck around; we need to check the man to see who he is and what his business on the road is at this time of night. He might be a terrorist for all you know."

They both knew that the man was no terrorist. They knew he was a small farmer, living with his mother, whose only goal in life was to get a wife and have a few pints. Moriarty braked and slewed the car across the road releasing an expletive list, which was not quite as exhaustive or colourful as Miklan's earlier tirade, as he did so. He cursed Miklan, the narrow road and the pedestrian as he slapped the steering wheel.

"FUCK YOU, FUCK THIS ROAD AND FUCK THAT FUCKING MAN WALKING."

He continued, "In the name of Jesus Christ are you mad? - for fuck's sake!"

Then he suddenly realised he was behaving like his colleague whose earlier display and loss of control did not appeal to him at all so he immediately shut up. He reversed to complete his three point turn and headed back towards the walking figure.

When they got to within thirty yards of the pedestrian the car slowed and the roof spotlight was switched on. The gardai caught a glimpse of the figure half running across the road and heading for the entrance to a farm lane. Leading on to the lane there was a narrow bridge with a low parapet. The car window was rolled down as they approached the fleeing figure.

Miklan jumped out waving his torch in the air and shouting, "Where to fuck do you think you are going in such a hurry at this time of night? I want a word with you."

As he approached the now stationary figure he proclaimed, "Jaysus sure you're not thinking of visiting anyone at this time of night man, everyone will be asleep in their beds."

Jim Sweeney stood on the bridge and turned to face the approaching figure who was shining his large garda torch directly into his face.

"What's the hurry? Ah it's yourself Jim."

He rasped breathlessly as he brought the torch to within three inches of the frightened face which recoiled with a grimace of terror.

"Now what was that you said to me last week when I asked you about the dog license? You know the law on dogs Jim; you know that every dog needs a license in this country."

As he spoke he jabbed the man in the chest with the torch. One vigorous jab per word.

"One-dog-one-license. Start with small law breaking and the next thing you are blowing up the police, you wouldn't be at anything like that would you Jim? All you cunts are the same, you might not be at it but you support them that are. I know you all."

He started jabbing the torch into his victim's chest once more saying, "You – know- what- I -mean -Jim ."

Again with a jab for each word, "Why have you gone all quiet?"

The man's silence seemed to cause an increase in the, alcohol fuelled, fury of the uniformed officer and his rage seemed to suddenly flare. The victim stood silent, helpless and seemingly paralysed with fear as he was subjected to further prodding and pushing with the torch. The garda sergeant appeared to want a reaction, perhaps to justify a further more intensive assault.

Then one of the more vigorous torch prods caught Jim Sweeney off guard and he lost his balance. His body fell backwards over the knee-high parapet of the bridge and down into the darkness below without a sound.

Miklan shone his torch down onto the dark surface of the rushing water torrent below to catch a glimpse of the struggling body now being carried downstream into the darkness. His first thought was to try and get him out but then he re-considered when he saw the impossibility of that task.

He realised the potential for trouble for himself. It would all come out, the drinking before going on duty, the assault on the innocent man – the lot. It would all come out and his career would end; no flats in Dublin, no retirement at fifty, the end of his dream.

Miklan walked hurriedly then started running back to the car with its headlights and roof spotlight still burning into the night. He opened the door that Moriarty had closed to keep out the night cold. He got in and his driver, who had been lying back relaxing with his eyes shut and his peaked cap tilted forward, straightened himself up and pushed back his cap. He opened his eyes wide when he heard the urgent tone in his colleague's voice.

Miklan spoke rapidly, "Turn off the spot, let's go, let's get to fuck out of here."

Moriarty straightened up fully forward when he saw the panic in his colleague's voice.

"What happened?" asked Moriarty who was now fully awake and alarmed at what he was hearing.

"The cunt only fell into the river." said Miklan.

"You mean you pushed him into the fucking river."

"No I never did, the cunt fell over the parapet, it was too low."

Moriarty jumped out of the car shouting, "Let's get him out."

"It's too late, he's gone, the river's too deep and fast there, he's gone I tell you. Look, let's get to fuck out of here. We saw nothing, a drunken man fell or jumped into a river, it happens all the time. There are no witnesses."

"No Miklan – for Christ's sake we can't just drive away and leave the man to drown."

"We can, we have to for Christ's sake, think about it!"

Moriarty grabbed the torch and rushed over to the bridge. He nearly fell over himself as he peered into the darkness with nothing to be seen by the light of the torch except the foaming water torrent.

He again shone the torch beam down into the water and along each bank. Nothing.

Miklan's face was full red and sweaty but turning white at the thought of what he had just accomplished. His mind raced........ 'What had happened? What had he done? It was an accident but he was involved, it would all come out, end of career, garda brutality, better say nothing, just turn around and drive on to Ballyleagh'. He spoke quietly and deliberately to Moriarty who was still trying to shine his torch and see something in the river.

"We saw no one or nothing. Look, there is no one about." said Milklan in a high pitched voice cracking with emotion and fear.

"For Christ sake Miklan there is a man drowning in the river there – does that mean nothing to you?"

"It's too late I tell you, he's gone, he's already dead, drive on, nothing happened."

By this time Miklan was back in and out of the car several times and peering again along the torch beam with his colleague.

"Look!" he roared, "If we don't get to fuck out of here soon someone will come and that will be it!"

Moriarty saw the sense in what he was hearing but he still could not take in the full horror of what had happened in the few short minutes since he, against his better judgement, had turned the car in the road. The two uniformed officers climbed back into their car and executed another three point turn and headed back towards their original destination.

Moriarty eased the car up the gears and picked up speed. The scene of the assault was soon receding into the November night. They drove on in silence until Miklan spoke.

"The cunt had it coming to him, you remember his ould chat last week about the dog and then the week before in the pub, that was him, the same boy, do you know his name – what was his second name? Well I guess it doesn't matter anymore – he's gone."

There was a long silence as Moriarty drove steadily along the winding road trying to figure out the best thing to do. Miklan seemed to be grinning in an inane manner.

"What are you talking about? he said fuck all to you, you were the one trying to get a rise out of him, it's not funny and if I was you I would worry, these things come out in the end and I am not sure if we should report it or not."

"ARE - YOU - MAD -? Nothing will come out if we saw nothing, you're involved too, you turned the car." said Miklan

"Just following orders sir."

It was 12.45am when both men straightened their ties and walked into the reception area at Ballyleagh garda station. The garda on desk duty barely looked up as they entered. He was one of the new postings to the area. New gardai were arriving weekly in response to the British requirement that security be beefed up to protect the stretch of the border from the southern side.

Miklan pondered what he was doing there at all in an attempt to reach some justification for his actions. - 'Wasn't there a need for it? Wasn't there a car bomb in Tirmore? The people felt safer now with all the guards and army about and a permanent checkpoint on the street. He was doing an important job for the country. Without him the whole place would collapse.'

Miklan knew that public opposition to the permanent security presence was soon squashed when the bomb arrived in their own village. He had little sympathy for the locals. It wasn't his job to wonder who had planted it. There was lots of conjecture in the garda about that - the Irish army or more probably they got the British army or their UVF agents to do it. Such considerations didn't matter at all to him because all the guard like himself wanted was lots of overtime and a good pay cheque every month. The work was boring but tolerable and the local girls saw a guard as a good catch with a safe job. He ran over all this in his mind but it did little to quell the rising panic in his entire body, the feeling in the pit of his stomach or the pounding of his heart. He thought it should have passed by now. He couldn't care less about his cup of tea and wanted to be on the road again. He couldn't sit still and relax. Moriarty was also restless but less so than his colleague.

After half an hour of restless resting the two guards turned their car towards Tirmore again. Soon they were driving past the spot on the road. Moriarty shook his head and pursed his lips.

"No good shaking your head, we were just doing our job."

 "Yeah there's a man dead in the river, is that our job? well I hope he's dead, better for you if he's dead."

"He was only a useless cunt."

"Cunt or no cunt, he's dead and you pushed him."

"Enough of that kind of talk, I never touched him, forget you saw anything. I have already forgotten."

Their shift ended at 8am in Tirmore Garda Station after they had completed their report for the night. No unusual events were recorded.

.

6 FALLING

Jim Sweeney was winded by the impact of the ten foot fall over the low bridge parapet and down into the water below but more severe injury was prevented because of the relaxed state of his body. The shock of the cold water soaking his back and legs soon overcame his alcoholic anaesthesia and caused him to leap up with his arms flailing and thrashing the water behind him in an attempt to gain a steady foothold in the slippery, stony bottom of the river. Thus was the energetic beginning of the struggle for survival that he would shortly lose.

Through the spray of the splashing water he glimpsed the light from the garda torch probing the darkness and the dark outline of the peaked cap moving against the starry night sky. He released a desperate, frightened cry for help followed by another which was strangled as the force of the river water swept him from his feet. Now on his back he was carried downstream by the rushing turbulent waters, his body was bumped over slimy stones as he struggled to stand upright, to grasp a hold of anything- a stone, a branch, a fistful of water. Rotating and tumbling to the left then to the right and soon wet through in the November cold. Now he was fifty yards downstream from the bridge where he entered the shadows of overhanging branches and into much deeper, quieter, faster flowing water that made no sound. Into the darkness.

All was silent around him apart from his own spluttering and gasping as the water was closing over him despite or because of his frantic struggle to keep afloat and to breathe. He could feel the weight of his wet clothes dragging him down and making any movement difficult. He could not swim which was a common failing in the people of Ireland. 'Shun the water because you might drown' was the only swimming lesson given in the catholic peasant houses and schools of Ireland at that time. His gulps of air got less frequent

Eddy Murray

and with every gasp more water than air flooded in through his open mouth and deep into his lungs. Soon a semi-asphyxiated calmness enveloped his body as he floated along through the cold, dark night. The struggling had ceased and his arms wafted freely alongside his body which was now moving at the whim of the rushing waters. The silhouette of trees became dimmer and the moon had gone.

His terrible cold and fear disappeared as his body and mind were suffused with warmth and a feeling of comfort. There was no awareness of the external cold which had now penetrated to the centre of his being. Quite suddenly he was floating in a dimly lit, warm room with Persian rugs hanging from the walls and deep white woollen carpets under him where he lay gazing up at a painted ceiling. There was a wild animal hunting scene depicted in shades of red and brown with a leopard carrying the lifeless body of a small deer by its neck. Then he was back in the bright glaring lights of a food factory in Kings Lynn sorting small potatoes on a moving belt with students from Belfast and their mealy, jarring accents around him, then watching a song of summer with a youth on the screen writing out music for a blind composer. The same youth was playing a game in the summer heat - throwing a ball across the roof of a brown brick country house with dense foliage on its walls and then running around the house to catch it as it tumbled from the roof. Just as quickly as it had come the scene changed to the hilly, rough road home from his first school. The clear view over to the heat hazed, blue mountain where he could see the distant smoke and grey-white steam from the railway engines coming down the mountainside hauling long cattle trains.   More sunny summer weather, twittering birds, the cuckoo summer song, wild strawberries in the hedge bank. There he was walking into the house to his mother and the dinner on the table with his brothers and sisters. The cloth school bag hanging over his shoulder then thrown on the ground. Flashing images and stories raced past.

'That boy is bright', the teacher said to his mother then it all changed again to spring time and he was struggling to unhitch a cart from a donkey so that he could tip out the load of cow manure. Manure was spread on the green, growing grass with a thin brown rope stretched between two sticks so that a straight potato ridge would result. Manure too fresh according to the anonymous neighbouring man who walked past and went on his way. The cart was emptied and the journey started to get another load across the way at the white house of the local dairy farm – older more mature manure next load, the resting brother now driving the cart with three helpers walking alongside. Then it was cold Christmas, a young boy was waiting at the railway station at the edge of the village, a small tin can filled with skimmed milk from the creamery resting on the ground. Gazing through the stout, white wooden bars of the railway gates closed to stop traffic as the train was coming. Two black cars waited alongside him with their engines running. He noticed the ribbed rubber on the running boards of the cars and his distorted reflection in the shiny, curved mudguard of the one nearest him. The train doors were banged shut by the guard, the whistle blew and the black train moved off slowly with a great fuss of steam and puffing smoke – then the stationmaster walked over and opened the gates, the cars moved off, his father had not come again so the boy picked up his can and the scene faded to be replaced by the glitzy glass mirror balls hanging in the semi darkness of the Dreamland ballroom. There was his father now still wearing his heavy winter coat and brown leather gloves in the heat of the kitchen, standing before a suitcase opened on the table and surrounded by children who moved away gleefully, clutching their Christmas presents – a black and white metal police car with the letters NY in gold on the front and back, a red plastic fire engine complete with ladders, a silver six gun, a blinking doll, a brown bear. Then he was in the school refectory dividing out yellow bread pudding from an oblong aluminium baking container. Biggest share for himself, the selfish server. There was the bald parish priest in front of the altar telling the faces before him that the life of Hollywood film stars was completely false. Then he was at his first communion in May time brilliant sunshine all fresh and renewed with his white shirt and grey short pants and red tie. The other seven year old boys were dressed in heavy dark brown, navy blue or grey suits with short trousers below the knee, 'yours is far nicer' said the local women to his mother who seemed embarrassed and made no reply. The girls were all dressed in long white laced gowns. Crisp childhood memories in minute detail flooded by. There he was again serving on the altar, lifting the priest's chasuble at the consecration and shaking the bell at each elevation, silent all silent now the noise had faded from his visual memories, the primary school room, a seven year old doing an essay for his best friend who couldn't write and getting slapped for the favour, the sadist lady teacher with the snipe nose then the   very kind and beautiful one, walking home on a cold and rainy days and a frosty starry night. Flip to summer meadows with the smell of new hay and tea with messy tomato

Eddy Murray

sandwiches and bread with blackcurrant jam, then the warm shelter of a brown hay stack on an exposed hillside and winter foddering, the angled reflection of hazel fishing rods appeared in calm lake waters, the bobbing cork and caught perch with rapidly arching and bending bodies struggling on the end of the line with protective fins uselessly deployed before dispatch with a sharp crack of a stick to the back of the head.

He woke briefly from his dream when his head struck a thick branch submerged in the river water close to the bank and he quickly realised where he was but not how he got there. He became aware of the extreme cold throughout his body and the water rushing around him. The desperate thrashing resumed but this time his heart was not in the struggle to live. He was too weak to will his heavy limbs to move in his own defence. Even in his weakened condition he realised the futility of further struggle, the cold was now fully established throughout his body and he longed to slip back into the warmth of his dream. Another final, weak gulp of watery air and he was gone again with the now silent flashing, dimmer images rotating faster, his mother, brother,sister, the road home, the pub, the blond smiling face of the long lost Gabrielle and the long forgotten Denise, the church, the graveyard, the open grave in the afternoon sun, the ancestral bones, the men washing the large crucifix, with outstretched flesh coloured body and red wounded side, in the spring well beside the church, the dance hall glitzy balls again, the lined up crowds of country girls, the barber cutting his hair with the new electric clippers, then a tin of dark tan shoe polish - Kiwi brand - came in to view and he could see the amber Kiwi body on the lid at the Saturday night children's shoe polishing that happened at the same time every week in preparation for Sunday mass. The long, pointed beak of the bird finally faded.

The force of the fast flowing river water had already started the task of disrobing the limp and lifeless body which floated semi-submerged in the foaming water. It removed the second shoe and was tugging at the trailing jacket, expertly and gradually undressing the body with each eddy and turn in the river. The sun was already starting its bright, frosty morning rise and displacing the dark.

The floating mass of the body was hindered here and caught there by stones or sticks jutting from the river bank or arching branches dipping into the water. Whatever the obstacle, the relentless water force won in the end and the remains of Jim Sweeney were carried onwards until the river current slowed as it merged with the broad Foyle. The body drifted to the shallows by the river bank. It came to rest in a reed bed under the green bridge where it remained until found on the third day of the manhunt. The dark, boggy river water continued to spill quietly into the Foyle on its journey back to the ocean.

It was 8.15 am on Monday 21 November 1976 and Jim Sweeney had been dead for seven hours. He was still not missing in his own home and life in the local community was starting up. The normal, uneventful, November day was just beginning. Half sleeping children hugged themselves in the morning cold on the yellow school bus as it headed for Ballyleagh. They had just passed the scene without noticing anything unusual except for the flooded fields caused by the heavy rain of the previous week. No one knew that a man's earthly walk had ended in the same river water – well no one who cared or was prepared to talk about it in any case.

Half a dozen black cattle drank water from the river pool beside the body, steam rising from their warm breath, but they paid no heed to the human drama which had reached its conclusion beside them. Two swans were busy a few yards out from the water's edge dipping their long necks into the water searching for edible material, in and out again and again with water dripping from their orange beaks filled with uprooted grass which they washed each time by swishing back and forth through the water before consumption.

This, sun filled, frosty November scene was repeated twice before the body was found. Each morning the rising winter sun cast long, bright gleams of yellow light through the dark green reeds and placed a pattern of lines across the upturned face of the near naked body floating there. The white shirt was the only item of clothing that remained attached to the body. It had been held in place by the tightly buttoned neck collar and floated behind and beneath his half submerged, upturned head. A shroud and pillow for a sleeping body.

Eddy Murray

7 MORIARTY AT HOME

Sergeant Mcgrath and Garda Moriarty were on the first bus out of Donegal after their shift had finished on the Monday morning. They were both in Dublin by noon having slept for most of the journey. Sergeant McGrath was going to his mother's home beside the Dodder river in Rathfarnam, a select suburb of south Dublin. Garda Moriarty took a Dublin taxi from Busaras - The Dublin Bus Station – to Prospect Avenue in the Glasnevin area on the north side where he still held a room in his parents' house looking out on John Kavanagh's pub. The north side of Dublin was considered less grand by the southsiders. Kavanagh's was more commonly known by the locals as The Gravediggers.

The gravediggers in question worked in the nearby Glasnevin cemetery which contained the mortal remains of many of the famous dead of Ireland such as the deceased members of the political classes like Daniel O'Connell, Michael Collins, Roger Casement, DeValera or O'Donovan Rossa whose graveside was the location for the famous 'The Fools. The Fools' pre-1916 oration by Padraig Pearse. Many literary figures including Brendan Behan and Gerard Manley Hopkins also have the cemetery as their last resting place. The fifteen foot grey-granite boundary wall of the cemetery ran across the bottom of Moriarty's garden.

On his days off Moriarty usually dropped his bag in his bedroom and after a short few words with his mother he would cross to the Diggers and spend the early afternoon catching up on local gossip and craic over a few pints. This would set him up for a few hours sleep before the start of the night-time revelry which was usually initiated with a pint or two and a game of snooker in the Garda social club. Having called at several refuelling stops on the way, the evening was always concluded in the company of one or more young females at the clubs of Leeson Street. Occasionally he would bump into

Eddy Murray

Sergeant McGrath and exchange a few words. The sergeant was a different age group and they had little in common on the social scene apart from a mutual interest in Aston Villa and The Dubs - the Dublin County Gaelic team.

As usual the barman greeted him with a few casual remarks about life up in the 'sticks' before offering him his customary drink – a pint of Guinness with a proper creamy, Dublin head. Moriarty did not feel much in the mood of talking but managed a few general comments about the pint on the border being as good as the Dublin version and a lot cheaper - with a grin to the barman. He nodded to a few acquaintances before he was once more immersed in his own thoughts about the events of the previous evening. His mood of heavy introspection was interrupted by a sharp slap on his back that caused him to jolt forwards and turn around to see the beaming face of Joseph Maguire who had been the fattest graduate in the class of 1975 and seemed to be still expanding with much straining of the buttons on his garda uniform jacket. Joseph was carrying his peaked cap under his arm . " Thought I'd find you here, what are you boys up to these days – how's life on the border?"

'Oh Christ.' thought Moriarty, 'just what I need ....'

"Oh, not bad, not bad, boring as hell but lots of overtime - what are you having? " replied Moriarty.

"I'm sticking to the water, starting at four today and on till midnight on the north side" He shuddered and continued, "I will need my wits about me around closing time tonight."

'A lot of good that fat cunt would be with or without his wits if things got sticky in the night' thought Moriarty. More useful behind a desk that fellow which was where he knew Maguire himself always intended to end up. He was just biding his time and keeping out of trouble on the beat before parking himself permanently in the station only to emerge in the most extreme emergency or at meal times. Fat gardai and women were known to be generally useless in street violence situations but had to be recruited through a non-discriminatory selection process. After a few more comments on life in general and gripes about the job Maguire tipped his glass on his head and drained the last few drops of Ballygowan still water and shards of clinking ice which he tried to dislodge from the bottom of the glass by repeated shaking and seemed determined to consume before departing. Once he succeeded in getting the last pieces of the ice from his glass into his mouth he proceeded to crunch them noisily and irritatingly.

Maguire did not buy Moriarty a return drink and Moriarty made a mental note of that for future reference as he watched the fat arse of Maguire easing itself out through the narrow half door of the pub. There were always people like Maguire who destroyed the pub culture of generosity by failing to buy their round. There were many ruses open to such round breaking miscreants. Somehow they usually managed to arrive in the company clutching a pint or when buying a round they might exclude their own. They could always make up a few pounds that way. Then there was the total bollix who simply never bought a round but that was a rare thing in Ireland whatever about other countries. He remembered one occasion in Dublin when he was drinking in company which included two North Korean diplomats. Now, maybe these two gentlemen thought it impolite to offer to buy a round or maybe even contrary to some North Korean custom to buy a drink when a guest in another country or whatever. While these two Orientals drank the Guinness with relish they failed to buy a drink all evening. Maybe they had no money.

Moriarty knew he was only using such round protocol deliberations to distract himself from the burning issue that lingered in his mind and flared up as the hourly news headlines came on the radio playing behind the bar. The Diggers did not allow television except for the all Ireland final. He was surprised that there had been no news announcement already because he knew the man had been missing now for over fifteen hours.

Had he been up in Donegal he would have been aware that the news of the missing man was just beginning to emerge locally at 2pm and there had still been no official involvement or announcement about the case. However it was the only point of conversation amongst the local population of Glenlackan since around three o'clock and it had reached North West Radio by four when a brief news item which was designated 'breaking news' reported that a local man had failed to return home after an evening out in Glenlackan. It also said that the Gardai had been informed and were keeping an open mind about the disappearance. The national radio station RTE was soon carrying the news with a first brief statement of the facts of the case on

Eddy Murray

the 5pm headlines. On the main 6.30 news there was a full report saying the gardai were still keeping an open mind and any information about the missing man was to be passed to Ballyleagh or to any Garda station.

"I wonder what happened to that fellow," said the Diggers' Dublin barman as he busied himself at his various bar tasks, drying glasses, wiping the counter, emptying the slops or running off the taps from the night before. He continued wiping as he spoke again, looking at Moriarty,

"Is that place not up near where you are stationed?"

Moriarty feigned a complete lack of interest and enquired where the incident had occurred before ordering another pint. He had intended to go home after the second one but for some reason - guilt, fear, or just to appear normal - he stayed on. There was now a danger that he might stay in the Diggers until closing time and it wouldn't be the first time his drinking had overcome his common sense. In the end he could no longer take the internal pressure of mentally rehearsing and reviewing the events of the night before so he downed his last half pint, eased himself off his wooden barstool and left with a brief, "See you" to the bar.

"Jaysus," said the barman shaking his head and addressing no one in particular, "must be something on that fellow's mind - I've never known the Moriarty lad so quiet"

" No," replied a regular standing with both elbows on the bar in front of a pint, "he's just tired, he was on patrol all night up around the border." The three customers in the bar nodded sympathetically and agreed he'd be back to himself after a bit of a sleep.

Moriarty decided to treat himself to a fish and chip in his favourite takeaway before going home for a sleep. He walked down past Hart's Corner to Forte's chip shop opposite The Brian Boru pub or Hedigans as it was locally known. He liked Forte's chips because they were nicely fried in palm oil and the fish was a decent size and not lost in excess batter. He finished the last bits of the fish supper while sitting on a picnic bench behind the Brian Boru and, feeling slightly re-energised, decided to take another pint before heading home. He knew he would be better going on home for a sleep immediately but was overcome by a sense of fatalism like a gambler who had just lost his money on the wheel and was determined to use the last coins to complete his destruction with drink - to become a complete loser.

Before he had left the bar the nine oclock television news told of a man called James Sweeney who was reported missing in Donegal. The news item asked for volunteers to report to the Dreamland ballroom at 8am the next morning to carry out a search of the area. Ominously the report included a mention of the flooded state of the local river. This did not help Moriarty's condition as he stared into his pint with the evening revellers starting to arrive at the bar. Normally he would be looking around at the young women parading themselves in various states of display and inebriation in front of him but not tonight.

The drink combined with his tiredness and secret knowledge seemed to conspire to create a mental condition that was most unpleasant. He knew he needed sleep and decided to make his way home. On his way he fumbled with thoughts about a way out of his predicament but every path took him to a dead end. He would have had no feelings of guilt about sinking that stupid bastard sergeant of his but knew that any admission at this stage would also immerse him in the affair. He was caught. He bitterly regretted not following his initial instinct to report the incident immediately and get a search organised for the victim. Who knows?, maybe he could have been saved.

His mother was surprised to see his generally dishevelled and distressed condition as she opened the door to admit her only son standing there in the darkness of the ivy hanging round the door. She had seen him drunk before but rarely so haggard. She put it down to overtiredness and reminded him that his blanket was on. Moriarty did not speak or look at his mother as he went up the stairs to his bed. He welcomed the warm caress of the electric blanket and was soon in the mercy of sleep.

When he woke the November sun was shining through the cream lace curtains on his window. He closed his eyes as if to shut out the reality that was streaming at him from all directions and seemed to be making its way through his mind and into the pit of his stomach where it lay like a bag of nails. He knew there was only one way out - full disclosure. He needed to have a chat with Miklan and was already constructing a scenario in his mind where he had not got out of the car at all and Miklan alone had cautioned the man about wearing an armband before leaving him on the bridge and continuing their journey to Ballyleagh. Even before he had this concocted he could see the holes in the story that would be visible to even the most incompetent and disinterested detective.

He got up, shaved, showered and dressed before making his way downstairs where his mother was making the dinner. He noticed it was already after eleven. "Well you had a good sleep," said his mother as she was wiping her hands in a towel and walked over to gently rub the back of her hand along the side of his face as he sat on the sofa. This caused him to pull away because he thought he was too old for that type of thing but in his distressed condition he did appreciate, for once, the mother's love that the caress represented. "That Sergeant McGrath was on the phone for you. I was a bit surprised because he doesn't usually call you at home. Said something about seeing you later at the social club."

Moriarty guessed what was on McGrath's mind and again regretted his woeful mistake. "Ah yes, old Miklan, he'll be wanting company for a dinner time drink and you know something, I just might not bother. I took one too many last night."

His mother looked at him wide-eyed and said with a laugh, "One?, I would say you took several too many, but that's the way when you fall in with company in Ireland."

"Yeah" replied Moriarty, "that's company for you."

He called Miklan and the two of them agreed to meet up at the Garda social Club at two that afternoon before heading up to Donegal for the start of their Tuesday night shift at 10pm. He noticed that his sergeant seemed particularly upbeat and almost ebullient on the phone. Could be bluff.

Mrs Moriarty made her son a fry because he announced he would not be around for dinner which was a disappointment to Mrs Moriarty who liked to sit and eat with him before he headed back to the wild north border.

8 MIKLAN AT HOME

Sergeant McGrath arrived at his mother's house around 1.30pm having called in for his car and a quick pint in the Garda Social club in Harrington Street close to Harold's Cross. He had left his car parked in the club grounds after an evening's socialising the week before because, by 1976, drink driving was becoming socially unacceptable in Ireland. He made his way to the bar where he expected to meet several of his graduating class enjoying a day off. Most of these were the lucky ones who had achieved what Miklan considered ideal, a Dublin posting.

There were the usual stories regarding ways of making money to augment the Garda salary. These included organising bouncers for clubs, security for the increasing numbers of celebrities arriving in Dublin and of course the well known landlord operations. Some gardai from his own class now owned several houses which they were renting out to students and other young people who could not afford the deposit to buy their own. One particular member of the force always seemed to be in the social club nursing a pint and knocking back brandies. This was the gambling arcade Garda and he seemed to have a very short working week. There was talk of 'connections'. He was the envy of his colleagues and could be looked on for a favour from time to time because he was becoming a man of increasing wealth and influence who seemed to have no problem mixing in the grey underworld of Dublin.

He left the club and drove directly to Rathfarnam and had just sat down after putting the kettle on for a cup of tea when his mother came home with a neighbour. "Welcome home John, this is my neighbour and best friend Mary Mullan. We play bingo together in the Parochial Hall every Monday dinnertime but we never, ever win." The two women set about laughing uproariously at this piece of high wit. "As I was telling you Mary, our John is

a very busy man keeping order on the border. A very responsible position"
Sergeant McGrath tolerated his mothers's rambling and recognised that she
was proud of her only son who "had passed all his exams with distinction in
the Garda College."

"Before I forget John, your Uncle Joe or should I say Superintendent McGrath
is keen to have a word with you, says he has something to tell you that might
interest you and you should give him a ring." Miklan was puzzled by this
message and knew it had nothing to do with his recent escapade in Donegal
which he had succeeded in dismissing as an inconvenient mishap that would
soon resolve itself. The only weak link in the chain was his car colleague,
Moriarty. He made a mental note to ring him and set up a meeting to make
sure he was still solid. When he rang he could only speak to the mother and
had to leave a message asking Moriarty to get back to him because the young
garda was already in the pub.

He rang his uncle and arranged to meet him in the Shelbourne Hotel at seven
that evening. Casual dress was suggested. He was puzzled about the uncle
and what he might want to tell him and the fact that he did not want the
meeting to happen in The Garda Social Club. When Miklan came back into
the living room the neighbour was getting up to leave. "Good bye Mrs
Mullan," said Miklan, in his most friendly and smiling voice, hardly able to
contain his glee that his uncle had set up a hotel meeting with him. Had to
be something important.

When the neighbour had left, Miklan shared his joy with his mother who
seemed equally delighted saying, "Well at least that is something your
useless father's family has been able to do for you, whatever it is. No thanks
to him though."

Unlike his two brothers Miklan's father had not joined the force but instead
had engaged in several business activities, none of which produced a profit.
He was more of a theoretical business man who could imagine any business
scenario and associated profits without the necessary acumen to assess its
real potential or the drive and sticking power to turn it into reality. You could
say he was the original poet - businessman. His mother had grown up on the
north side and the house in Rathfarnam had been left to her by a maternal
aunt.

Soon the mother was busy telling Miklan that the Dodder River had been in flood for the past two weeks and every time it happened it flowed across the bottom of her garden leaving a mess of rubbish and dirt. People upstream, which included a travellers encampment, saw the river as a useful receptacle for all types of waste of organic or inorganic composition. She had been in contact with the council but they said it was a problem that had been recurring for the past hundred years. Miklan walked down to the river bank and surveyed the flood zone with its rim of paper, wood, plastic and material of indeterminate composition which looked unpleasant and had a decidedly sewage type odour and hue. For a moment the fast flowing waters produced a minor flashback to the previous night's events but this was quickly replaced with practical matters regarding the contamination and its solution.

Miklan returned to the house and told his mother that the way to approach the problem was as a health and safety issue. This was the only way to get something done because, once alerted, the Council was obliged to take action or face a court case which they would be bound to lose. He told his mother to suggest that the council needed to build a wall to retain the flood waters within the river banks at the bottom of her garden which was the only house affected. Mrs McGrath was intensely proud of her son's brilliance and she felt reassured by his precise solution to her flooding problem. She saw this as further proof of his abilities.

Miklan put on his best casual which included some fine golfing gear with the logo of Pebble Beach Golf Club that he thought should impress the superintendent uncle. He had played a couple of rounds there on his last visit to San Francisco or more accurately Palo Alto where his cousin had married an American who had, by good fortune and smart investment, become and remained a millionaire with a lifestyle to match. Nothing ostentatious, just the best - hotels, golf courses, friends, clothes, cars, hunting trips and such like.

He entered the Horseshoe bar of the Shelbourne Hotel on Stephen's Green at 6.45pm, looked around to ensure his uncle was not there already then lifted a newspaper from the rack and sat down, pretending to read while he waited. The waiter came over but, unusually, Miklan said he would wait until his guest arrived.

Eddy Murray

When the uncle did finally arrive at 7.23pm he was in the company of a dark suited gentleman that Miklan did not recognise. He should have known this man because he was the person in overall charge of security on the border. Miklan stood up to be introduced by his uncle who said, "John, this is Mr Donegan, The Minister for Defence." Miklan was taken aback by the height of the state official he was now shaking hands with but soon recovered and knowing he was resting on his family laurels, said, "I am very pleased to meet you Minister and thank you Superintendent for arranging this meeting but I have to say I am in the dark as to the purpose."

"All in good time, it will all become clear shortly and call me Paddy," said the minister in a thick Louth accent that Miklan would have usually referred to as 'culchie', but not of course when a Minister of the Irish State was speaking. The three men were just taking their seats when a waiter arrived, silver tray in hand. The superintendent did the ordering, brandy for himself and pint of Guinness for Miklan and the minister. There followed about five minutes of small talk including a mention of the excellent Pebble Beach Club and the quality of the facilities there. Miklan was secretly exulting in his choice of jumper and felt his uncle would be proud of him and impressed with his quality associates. He was right. Here, thought the uncle, was obviously a man with a good corporate image and ability to mix in the highest circles – just the kind of man the minister needed for the job which was going to be the subject and purpose of the meeting.

The minister signalled the end of the small talk by clearing his throat loudly after taking a large swig of Guinness. Looking directly at Miklan he said, "I have a small problem in Donegal that you might be able to help me with. Well, in fact, it might be widespread all along the border but certainly I am getting whispers of irregular events and a few difficulties on the ground up there in Donegal where you are based. I have been given your name by your superiors and you come highly recommended." At last thought Miklan, someone has recognised my diligence in upholding the law which many do gooders and liberals were likely to call harassment of the local population.

In fact no superior had recommended Miklan, his name had been given to the minister by the uncle and this opportunity for the nephew was a payback for past favours involving the quoshing of several drink driving charges. This is how things are done in Ireland at all levels but especially amongst the political classes.

The minister continued, "I have responsibility for all the armed forces of this country including, of course, the large combined section of the defence forces deployed along the border in support of the civil authority - the gardai. I need a liaison officer on the ground who can apprise me of the situation as it is happening with respect to the army operating alongside the gardai. I need someone who knows the ropes and will be able to act independently to identify and, if possible, sort out any operational difficulties that might arise from day to day. You will be reporting directly to me and will be in post at the level of Inspector. The rank will be temporary initially but will be made permanent after six months in the job." Miklan liked what the minister was saying, he liked it very much indeed.

The superintendent looked at Miklan saying, "How does that sound to you?" "Sounds great," replied Miklan, and warming to the sound of his own voice continued, "this is exactly the kind of role I would have envisaged for myself with a good degree of operational independence and elements of trouble shooting. If I read you correctly," looking at the minister, "this is primarily a managerial role with potential for improving the service to the people and of course to the country."

"Couldn't have put it better myself," said the minister nodding and smiling while the superintendent was positively beaming at his nephew which reflected the condition of Miklan's own inner being. At last he thought, I am going to make it – now we will see who will have the broadest smile in the next photo of his friends from the class at Templemore.

"Where will I be based ?" queried Miklan. The minister answered after a short pause, "In Dublin mostly but you will be spending time at the army headquarters in The Curragh and locally at Finner in Donegal. On the Garda side you will have liaison responsibility for all Garda stations in Donegal and will have access to all reports, premises and operational plans. Of course all hotel and travel expenses will be met whenever you are away from your Dublin base and you will have the use of an unmarked Garda car. We may expand the role after a six monthly review and then of course it is likely that you will need an assistant and a secretary." Miklan thought it was beginning to sound better by the minute and such was his joy that he felt his body was defying gravity and floating upward from his seat.

Eddy Murray

As if on cue the superintendent had to go to the toilet whereupon the minister moved closer to Miklan's ear. He could feel and smell the minister's warm breath which made him feel a little uncomfortable but he did not recoil as the minister half whispered. "Fact is we are getting reports that some Garda officers and possibly Army personnel are getting too close to the IRA. I cannot put it any plainer nor can I overemphasise the need for accurate information on the status of any such linkages. The stability of the state itself is in jeopardy. You must remember we have had the national disgrace and embarrassment of the murder of the British ambassador right here in Dublin five months ago. We suspect inside information and possible involvement. Your official role will be as garda-army liaison officer but you now know the full ramifications of the post that only you and I are aware of."

The minister paused and sat back as Miklan's mind grappled with the full importance of what he had just heard. The uncle returned from his toilet break and the minister leaned forward to speak. "Unfortunately I have to rush to my next meeting or I would have enjoyed another pint with you. I look forward to your first report and expect regular updates and one on one briefings. You will be acting under your own initiative."

Just as quickly as he had come the minister had shaken all hands and departed. The superintendent was now able to focus on Miklan who was starting to enjoy his second pint. "You'll be needing less of that stuff for the foreseeable future. Know what I mean?" then continued, "Of course it goes without saying that this meeting did not happen and you know nothing about any upcoming liaison post. The position will be advertised in the internal job opportunities bulletin and you will apply in the usual manner. Needless to say if you decide to apply the job is yours. Well how do feel now Inspector? This is your first step on the ladder. Your father will be proud of you if he ever does show up again."

As Miklan was driving away from the Shelbourne meeting and into the next day his thoughts focussed on one issue - the absolute necessity for Moriarty to keep his mouth shut and to stay on message regarding the previous Sunday night. There was more riding on this now and he felt satisfied that there would be no hiccups because it was in Moriarty's own interest to stick with the original story.

The next day's meeting with Moriarty got off to a shaky start when the junior garda seemed inclined to change his version of events. "How about if I say I remained in the car and you alone went to speak to the pedestrian about his armband" said Moriarty to Miklan in a quiet corner of the social club. Miklan nearly exploded with rage but glancing around noticed others close by and contained himself and his grimace of impatience turned to a smile as he whispered, "Ah for Jaysus sake not at all, that would never do, that would be so unbelievable that the truth would be out in minutes and don't forget that would have serious consequences for yourself too. No, No, all we have to do is keep with the version where we returned and the pedestrian had disappeared by the time we arrived at the point on the road where we had seen him walking without an armband. For Christ's sake. We have to keep it simple."

At the end of their shift on the Wednesday morning, Miklan and Moriarty reported their sighting of an individual on the road on the previous Sunday night. Superintendent Mehaffy listened to their account including the fact that they had been visiting relatives in Dublin over the intervening two days and were totally unaware of any search operation for this missing man. The superintendent asked them to make a full written report to be presented to him personally.

9 MISSING

Anne Sweeney turned in her bed and looked towards the lighted dial on her electric alarm clock on the side table. The wooden table was covered in a white cotton cloth that she had embroidered with flowers of many colours still visible in the low glow from the clock. The time was 3.33am. She wondered briefly why she had not been awake or awakened when Jim returned earlier. She usually heard him making his way down the hall to the kitchen to get a bite to eat and satisfy the hunger in a man that is always brought on by alcohol. She had endured the same pattern in her husband before he finally departed.

She often wondered what life would be like with a man who didn't take alcohol and why this type of drinking behaviour was so common in Ireland that it seemed almost part of being Irish. She had often heard Father McCarney speak about it in his sermons, he called it the curse of the Irish and all the women in the chapel who had men drinking in the house knew the truth of that. She wondered what the attraction of alcohol was, not the occasional drink or two but the regular visit to the pub every weekend.

She reached for her rosary beads on the side table and drew them from the cold air into the warmth under the blankets. Saying a decade of the rosary was a common practice among Irish women whenever anxiety was creeping towards the conscious mind and she had said the five decades of the rosary every night in the house when the family was growing up. 'The family that prays together stays together' was the slogan from Father Peyton, the rosary priest from Mayo. Well it had not worked for her family. Her husband had been killed ten year earlier when he was trapped under an overturned tractor in Luton. That was the news that had been brought to her on that day she would never forget. Two old school pals arrived on the street with that look on their face. She simply said to them 'Who is it?' and waited for the blow to fall.

His death and burial in England did not bother her after a time because she had got used to being the manager in her own house and he had always seemed to resent that, whenever he was home on holidays. However she did miss the money and times were hard, living on the small state handout. She had managed somehow.

He had been a good man, a hard working man who was useful but he never seemed to want to settle down in the family home. Mind you he always sent the money faithfully every week which was commented on by the postman as she signed the registered envelope receipt on Tuesday mornings. The postman was one of the few callers at the house where she lived in semi-isolation from the local community. Now the memory gates were fully opened and the undammed thoughts came pouring in as was usual in the small hours.

The happy times when she was a lively eighteen and playing the accordion in the small dance band, with her brother on the drums, cousin on the fiddle, and desperate for companionship and wondering if everyone felt the same. The crushing inner feelings of loneliness and then the men. The men got what they wanted and moved on.

She lingered fondly on her youthful experiences with men while playing on the US army base across the border during the war. She loved the yanks because of their openness, their generosity and their laughter which was so different from the dour, dark and damp locals with their midden depths. Then one day, quite suddenly they were gone - all gone, their tents were lying empty behind the wire netting fence. There was talk of the invasion of Europe. She had one particular young man in mind, an eighteen year old boy was all he was and she often wondered if he would ever come back. She could still see his smile and hear his broad American drawl that she loved. Jim McCann and Wyoming seemed so appealing, so romantic. So far away and so good to escape to. He didn't return and she had to be content with the locals who would expect that she had learned some new tricks with the Yanks and may be considered tainted by the experience.

Funniest thing was, well not funny at all, but something she found peculiar. The local ones she was most intimate with in every sense seemed to ignore her most completely the next night or the next week or the next month as though it never happened. A shameful episode to be ignored. Well, all except Joe, the man who married her when she fell pregnant and he wasn't even the father. It was his brother, the man around town of the family who could charm the women but then, like the rest, did not want to know. Nobody ever mentioned this twist in the tale but she knew and always suspected that they knew because public house chat is always about things like that. The public houses of Ireland are filled with the most inquisitive, most twisted and loneliest people.

Then the futile frantic race to get married away from the locality but the neighbours knew, oh yes they knew alright and the brother was not slow to tell them. Men dropping sly hints about knowing her or whistling as she rode past on her pushbike even twenty years later. The miserable bastards never forget their conquest of a woman that meant they knew her forever, an object of shame and derision, and an easy mark. What a horror. The shout across the dimly lit village street from a pimply, pubescent son of some local cattle jobber 'Would you like a ride Anne?' Why had she not run far and fast away? To where – to anywhere would be better than this and yet she stayed in a display of courage or foolishness. She was still undecided about that and anyway it depended on her mood.

They were mostly all departed now but still it hurt. The anger and hurt, the shame anger and hurt and guilt whatever that was. The local curate said all was forgiven – all what exactly? Another priest, the parish priest, a stern man, had said it might be better to go away to England if necessary because-

'You and your children will always walk this neighbourhood with downcast eyes and what about your poor husband?'

She could never erase those words from her memory and they came back in exactly the same form, word for word every time the dam burst.

'What about your poor husband?'

He had also kept saying something about lasting damage to 'Our way of life and to Irish society.'

But she never fully understood that. Then he followed up this verbal onslaught with- 'Getting married was a mistake, it never works out, better for you and the child to have gone to a home run by nuns down in Dublin, child and yourself well looked after. Then after a suitable period of penance you could safely re-enter society with the child adopted.'

Yes these thoughts came back every night that she couldn't get to sleep in the long and lonely hours. The same ones, round and round they went and in a way she enjoyed them despite the horror of her life replayed in the dark night. The only way to stop the flood was to pray but there was no guarantee that this would always work. The decades of the rosary, what a tortured life, why is the mind so troublesome then in they flooded again.

The period in England just before the war where she hated her work in the hospital as a trainee nurse, a skivvy more like. She saw the working class women coming in with their hair filled with lice and thought the working class and the poor were badly treated there and she resolved to get back to her father's house in Ireland and never return. The war was about to break out and her brother organised a letter saying she had to come home because her mother was ill. This was to ensure the authorities would let her go home to Ireland, what with the war effort and all that.

Her decision never to return to England was not very welcomed especially by the brother-in law, the mother's 'white haired' boy of the family because the farm would have to be split. He was a good talker but no worker. What a choice and she took the only one she thought she could. She decided to face it, to stay in the area and live in the middle of the horror and shame, the shame and horror, the horrible horror, the shame.

 Joe built a house. He was a worker and things were alright but the neighbours' rejection started shortly afterward when he had returned to England to find work. By now she had four children and another on the way. She was determined that they would get an education but first they had to be fed. Milk was essential. All the neighbours kept cows and she naturally assumed that they would have no problem selling her a pint or two of milk every day. Well she was wrong. First the closest ones refused but then as she cycled on to another, and another the rejections came. So that was how it was done, eviction by isolation. The cowards, she was a woman alone with four children under six. In desperation and alone, and not for the first or last time, she wanted to gather up her children and run back home to her father's house but how long could that last before she was having a row with him again. She had always accused him of being a lazy good for nothing who left all the work of the farm and inside the house to her own mother.

Then she remembered her joy when one mile away a gentle soul called Hugh agreed to supply her daily needs for milk and went further and she always remembered his kindness and his words came back as a moment of sweetness in her life;

'You are always welcome to have milk here for as long as you want and there is no need to pay.'

Her eyes still filled up with tears every time she remembered. The thoughts always breached her carefully constructed barriers of mental toughness. But she would not hear of it and paid the man every day for the milk she took in her small tin can. She knew it was no small thing to be seen associating with a tainted woman in the locality especially since the priest had strongly advised her to go, to leave us in peace. His words came back again.

That was when she got the idea of getting a goat to avoid the daily journey for milk with her children left behind alone in the house. A goat because a man would be needed about the house for calving so a cow was out of the question and a goat would be easier managed. But now this goat was another source of shame and open to derision. The goat was a poor man's cow. This generation of Ireland's Catholics were getting back to farming after the years of oppression, any man with cattle and land was looked up to and the more cattle he had the higher he was.

Goats were a source of shame but she did not care because by this time she had turned completely to Jesus as her only support. She recalled her time with the goats as a time of hope with the children growing up - the years before the failures.

The last goat had been left tethered outside by accident one night and had been savaged by a pack of dogs or wild animals. Its belly had been ripped out. The rosary beads and Jesus, Mary and Joseph became her guardians. This might have been fine but for the fact that she seemed to be thinking more often that the Catholic Church was not exactly Christian. She soon discovered that the church in Ireland leaned towards the well off. The ordinary priests mostly came from the poor but seemed to despise their origins. Not the first time that sort of thing had happened in Ireland but she had expected more from the church. The one source of truth in the world.

Now after all that her whole family scattered to the winds and the wild, Birmingham and further. Still she felt lucky to have her youngest son Jim who had returned home to look after the family farm. But this was also an admission of failure. More shame because she had hopes for the youngest son. That he might be a priest or a doctor. He was bright enough and so every penny was saved and he was sent on to secondary school and university. So why was he back living at home, the questions came from neighbours indirectly, slyly.

The garage man mentioned how he had seen him up and down the road with the schoolbag on his back for years and left it there. Just that, up and down the road with a school bag on his back, the words repeated in her mind. There was no suggestion of a statement other than the observation so she was left with her own mind to fill in the blanks,

'So he has failed then and I never went to school and I am doing very well.'

Oh yes those were the blanks alright and many of them, a close knit community all right. Full of blanked out meaning, sly hidden abusive meaning, intrusive meaning. Ireland of the sorrows, the sly abusive sorrows, the horrible, holy terrorising sorrows. Then there was her daughter Marilyn who was married with a family, six mile down the road. Married to Damian, a small farmer, same as herself but without any inclination to do the work just like her own father. The man the daughter had married was a good man but a lazy man who just liked chatting and joking, he surely was good craic. She never allowed herself to think about her eldest daughter who had left home for America after a row. She had made terrible, false accusations against a priest who had been visiting the area when she was fifteen - and yet? No, No. No.

Her thoughts turned again to the youngest son. Well the education didn't work out for him and she recalled how five years earlier he had spent a short time in England canning vegetables in a factory in England before returning home at the end of the summer. Of course all the neighbours seen his return as final proof of failure because it was September and he was not returning to college or to a job. Yet another dull thud, yet one more. All the other sons as labourers on the buildings in England, still they all had their own families and seemed happy. They returned once a year to visit at Christmas or during the summer months and sometimes help at the hay, a strangely punishing ritual trying to dry hay in the valley of rain. She often thought and said that England was a great country. More often the time at home was spent in the pub which was a habit learned from their father when he was alive and around. The same with Jim. He seemed to need and see the frequent pub visit as more important than the church on Sunday. The money was scarce and drinking seemed a total waste and besides it made them cranky. Still what could you do, pray because Jesus never lets you down or that's what she was told from her childhood days.

Putting yellow May flowers on the doorstep to welcome the blessed virgin Mary who was supposed to call at houses on the first day of May or the multiple church visits praying for departed relations on all souls night at Halloween. The clear images of these two times of year came fresh to her mind amongst the jarring, painful, jumbled stories that made up the rest of her thoughts that she now had enough of. She wanted to and tried to banish them as she went through the ten Hail Marys and the Hail Holy Queen followed by numerous beseechings on behalf of all the dead, her own mother, her husband despite the fact she never liked him that much. She had fancied his brother but better not dwell on that again.

Then it began again - the thought of her youngest son drinking in the pub and rubbing shoulders with those men, the few that were still living around the area and so it went on. She tried to remember if she had told him to get the dog license and show it at the station to stop 'them guards' calling at the house. She made up her mind to tell him again first thing in the morning. Between aspirations, prayerful beseeching and racing thoughts she drifted back to sleep.

It was ten in the morning before she woke and got up to a cold house. Jim must have gone out without lighting the fire. That was unusual but maybe someone called, maybe a neighbour's cow was calving. So she broke the cipins herself and poured a small amount of red diesel on two long, dry pieces of hardened black turf before applying the match. The fire started with the yellow flames shooting upwards, smoky, sooty. She rubbed her hands before it to get the full benefit of the heat then put two shovels of coal on top before closing the cooker door. She walked into the scullery and started to fill the kettle at the sink there. It had been a frosty night and the cold had got into the house.

She thought it strange that Jim had not touched any of the food left over from the Sunday dinner. It was as she had left it the day before. Normally everything was devoured with a mess left behind. He was not in the house but she was not surprised or worried. It was not that unusual for him to be out because he was an early riser and the neighbours said he could often be heard out clattering and banging across the hill at a very early hour. But that was usually in spring or summer and not in the cold November when the only activity on the small farm was cutting sticks and giving a bit of hay to the remaining calves and the cows who would be due to calve again around February .

She washed and peeled enough potatoes for dinner for the two of them and cut and washed a half head of cabbage. Very meticulously each piece of cabbage was examined for crawling life under a running tap. The meat today would be a piece of bacon cut from the smoked side hanging there. After two hours in the oven that would make a tasty bite with some left over for his supper or lunch tomorrow.

The chickens were still locked up so she opened them and gave them a few handfuls of meal mixed with boiled potato peelings. It seemed to work well because she had the best laying hens in the country and could make a few pound selling the spare eggs. These were rare hens because most hens had stopped laying in September or October with the non-laying period lasting until things warmed up in spring.

She cycled the half mile to the priest's house to prepare his dinner and leave it in the oven for him. She had her own key and let herself in to the parochial house.

By one clock she was back in her own kitchen and had put her son's dinner on the table but there was still no sign of him. She took her dinner plate to her usual position in the armchair in front of the fire. When she had finished eating she started to wonder where he was. She went outside and checked the outhouses. She thought it strange that Rover, his dog, was still closed in the shed because that dog always went everywhere with Jim on the farm.

Her imagination had not yet reached the level of worry but it was building. Down the road to the neighbour's house – "No Mrs Sweeney – he's not here." then another, "no sign". Now it was in full fling. The ravages of worry raced through her mind. Back up to the house to check his bed and dreading what she might find. She found nothing - the bed had not been slept in. Jim Dolan, her nearest neighbour, was in the kitchen having checked the outhouses again. No sign, a mystery, frantic worry now taking hold, the beads came out again, get the priest, get the guards. The mile long cycle down to the village to the telephone took forever - 'Where is he? Where could he be?'

His uneaten dinner sat on the table covered with a white tea cloth.

10 FOUND

The local newspaper report was brief. After an extensive search lead by Garda McDonald from Ballyleagh station the body of local man Jim Sweeney was found. It had been located in the River Lackan approximately two miles downstream from Glenlackan Cross which was the last reported sighting of the deceased alive.

It was 2.00pm on Wednesday 23 November 1976 and the land search for the missing man was about to be called off. The gardai were of the opinion that they would have to bring in the sub-aqua squad to conduct a search of the river itself. The discovery was made by a neighbour called John Magauran who let out a simple shout – here he is - when he saw the outline of the half submerged, blue white body floating in the shallow water amongst the reeds. The cattle at the water's edge took fright at the sudden shout and rush of searchers to the spot. They stampeded, hooves thudding up the field before stopping at what they considered a safe distance to stand and gaze backwards before starting to advance closer in a line of curious beasts towards the increasing crowd of searchers.

"Here he is!" This was the simple, shouted statement that alerted those around him and partially ended the mystery of the disappearance of Jim Sweeney three days earlier.

When he did not turn up for his dinner on the Monday his mother became alarmed and alerted the neighbours. A search of farm buildings and fields had been completed by his mother and neighbours who believed that he may have gone out early in the morning to look at cattle and at worst may be lying injured in a field after a fall or maybe even an attack by cattle. This type of attack is common enough because he may have had his dog with him and cattle often attack a dog taking refuge behind his owner who then

Eddy Murray

becomes the object of the beasts' attention. In fact his dog was still closed in his shed where Jim had left him before he went to the pub the night before. When this search proved fruitless the priest and the gardai were alerted.

He was officially declared and confirmed as a missing person at 6.00pm on Monday 21 November by Garda McDonald who had been assigned to the case. The, navy blue Hillman Avenger, garda car drove on to the street and a single uniformed garda emerged. It was already getting dusk and Mrs Sweeney was becoming increasingly frantic and kept urging the garda to find her son. However the garda was not going to be diverted from his professional investigation of a missing person by any emotional outpourings. He reminded the distraught mother that everything possible would be done to find her son but first enquiries had to be made to establish the circumstances of the disappearance and exactly where he had been last seen. He reassured her that ninety nine percent of missing people were not missing at all but were away for some simple reason. He knew that he must immediately begin a systematic questioning of the mother, relatives and neighbours to try and construct a timetable of events since the missing person had last been seen.

The black and white sheepdog, usually the first to announce the arrival of a newcomer on the street, seemed peculiarly subdued and remained silent as if it too was concerned. The dog simply sat on the street with its head cocked to one side and ears alert and waiting for someone or something. The day was unusual insofar as he had not seen his master. Usually the sheepdog would be Jim's companion as he worked about the yard or walked the land carrying out simple winter tasks like mending fences or cutting timber. This was an outdoor dog that rarely entered the house.

"Now Mrs Sweeney," the garda officer began, "let us go inside to the kitchen until I ask you a few routine questions."

By this time Marilyn, the sister of the missing man, her husband Damian, and son Edward were getting out of a yellow mark three Cortina that had driven onto the street. Marilyn rushed over to the open door of the house where her mother had appeared and hugged her saying, "Isn't it awful - I'm sure he'll be found safe – I'm sure he will."

The mother was shaking her head, "I'm not so sure - but please God he will."

The garda came out into the hall and intervened, saying. "Look, it's getting dark and we really do need to establish the facts of the case so that we can begin a proper search if this man really is missing and has not turned up before morning."

He ushered the mother and sister back into the kitchen while the men stood outside on the street talking quietly in the gathering gloom. The garda removed his peaked cap and placed it on the table before sitting down on a rung backed wooden chair at the same time as he was withdrawing a small notebook and pencil from the breast pocket of his silver buttoned tunic. He turned sideways in the chair so that the light from the single electric bulb, which was hanging in the middle of the ceiling, shone directly onto his notebook now resting on the table and said quietly, "Let me see now Mrs Sweeney." He paused and clicked his pen before continuing, "You say the first you knew that your son was missing was when he failed to turn up for his dinner at one o'clock today."

"Yes," replied the woman pointing at the covered dinner plate still sitting on the table. Her reply was delivered with some impatience because she had already told him this at least twice before. What the woman did not realise is that an investigating garda asks the same question several times to check if the facts remain consistent.

"Did you notice if his bed had been slept in?"

Mrs Sweeney looked away and towards her daughter.

"Mrs Sweeney," said the garda, "was his bed slept in?"

"To tell you the truth I couldn't tell you if it had been or not. Jim was not in the habit of making his bed. But when I went up to look when he didn't turn up for his dinner he wasn't there and the bed wasn't made but that would not be unusual."

This questioning puzzled the mother who seemed to think that someone should be taking steps to find her missing son. Mrs Sweeney looked over at her daughter and then towards the Garda officer. "You know how he was,

Eddy Murray

how all men are."

The garda smiled and nodded his head. "I understand, but as far as you are aware he did not come home last night."

As she pointed with her raised hand she replied. "I did not hear him coming in and my bedroom is on the ground floor, over there. I always hear him rooting about in the kitchen, he usually makes a bite to eat before he turns in, especially if he had been in the pub."

The officer nodded knowingly before continuing his line of questioning,

"Was there any suggestion that the missing man had made any plans to leave home for any reason whatever. For example did you have a row? Was he depressed?"

The garda noticed the woman in front of him was taken aback by the last questions and was aware of the reticence of people in talking about such matters and he spoke softly, "I'm sorry Mrs Sweeney but you must understand I have to establish the facts of every case."

Mrs Sweeney nodded her head saying – "I know that garda, I know that but we had no row and he never goes away without saying where he is going. Was he depressed? no, not that I noticed."

Mrs Sweeney looked over at her daughter who nodded in confirmation.

The garda kept writing, "and you say the last time you saw him was when he left this house to go for a drink to the pub at 8pm on Sunday evening."

Again the mother nodded and whispered – "yes that's right – the last time" - as her voice trailed to a whisper. "Around eight last night."

Garda McDonald rose from the table.

"OK thank you Mrs Sweeney – I understand your concern but as I said most missing people do turn up. That is all I need at the moment but rest assured that the Garda Siochana will do everything in its power to find your son and return him safely to you. You can be sure of that. All garda and army patrols will be alerted and will carry out searches in this area by torchlight. We will try to get something on the nine o'clock television and radio news and the local radio. The more we can publicise this the better. It is getting dark now so we will not be able to start a full search until morning light. Hopefully all that will not prove necessary and if the situation changes I will immediately inform you and I would appreciate if you would ring me at the station if you find out anything relating to this missing person."

Mrs Sweeney hugged her daughter and was close to tears but felt reassured that the forces of the state were now fully engaged in helping to find her son.

Garda McDonald replaced his cap on his head as he was leaving the house and walked towards the patrol car with the dark blue police lamp on top. He noticed that there were now six men standing in a pall of cigarette smoke under the yellow glow of the yard wall light. He nodded towards them as he passed. He stopped to say that he would be continuing his enquiries and the security forces would be carrying out a limited search throughout the night but if any information came to light he would appreciate if they telephoned the station immediately.

"I have left the number in the house. If we have to conduct a wide search we will need volunteers – in the morning. We will make final arrangements later on this evening. Listen to the radio for any announcements."

The owner of the local pub was able to tell Garda McDonald that the missing man had indeed left his licensed premises around 11.00 and had set out to walk home as was his custom. The doorman at the Dreamland ballroom knew Jim Sweeney well and was able to confirm that he had not entered the hall that night.

Announcements on the Monday evening news on the radio and television delivered the facts of the case. The gardai were keeping an open mind with regard to the missing man but a full search would be resumed at first light. Local people who wished to assist in the search were asked to assemble at the Dreamland ballroom at eight o'clock the following morning.

So began the search for the missing man. Fifty local men were in the hall at the appointed time when the door swung open and Garda McDonald marched in followed by ten other gardai, five part time members of Tirmore fire brigade in their navy uniforms, ten army cadets and two lecturers in charge of about twenty students from the local agricultural college who had volunteered to join in the search. About 100 searchers in total.

Garda McDonald was experienced in water sports and outdoor activities which was why the station superintendent selected him to organise the search. He unfolded a map on a small table in front of him and addressed the assembled people.

"First can I thank you all for coming out so early on such a cold morning, it is vital to get this search organised and underway quickly because of the limited hours of daylight. I have divided the map into ten search districts, each to cover an area of approximately four square miles. We will split up into groups with about a dozen people in each. A garda officer will lead each group. Because the river is in flood we will initially concentrate our search along its length on both sides and about one hundred yards out from each bank. But each general search area will eventually cover a part of the river bank extending to a distance of half mile from it.

We need to be meticulous in our search and there is urgency to things because this man may be lying seriously injured or suffering from hypothermia in this area. I am aware that many of these have been searched already in the night but pay particular attention to old farm buildings that are not in regular use. If this man is still alive he must be found and found soon. Hopefully the search will have a quick and successful outcome before then but I have organised with the ICA to provide soup and sandwiches at 1pm in the hall here and each group will be transported to and from its assigned search area by army vehicles. I wish you luck in your search – has anyone any questions? Father McCarney you have a question?"

Fr McCarney rose to his feet, "Not really a question just to say that I offered up a mass this morning so that this search would have a happy outcome." "But,"..... and he seemed lost for words... "if the worst comes then it is important that I be summoned immediately to anoint the body. The family would want this."

"Thank you father, indeed we all understand the feelings of the family and I would ask all involved to bear in mind what you just heard in the unlikely event that this search does not find a live person. Now I would ask you to join one of the garda who is positioned around the room. They have their orders and will lead you to your search area."

James McCarty, the local postman, wanted to know how each group could stay in touch and was told that each group would be accompanied by an army radio officer who would report in regularly to the central control base which will be this hall. "All units will be updated from here."

"Any more questions or comments?" Asked Garda McDonald in the expectation that there would be none - he was wrong.

A voice came from the back of the crowd. "I am Mr O'Donlon and I would like to know what provision has been made for any insurance for the civilian searchers in the event of any injury sustained in the course of our activities on this search operation."

Garda McDonald's face registered astonishment tinged with slight impatience and he paused for a moment before replying. "While I can understand your concerns I do not envisage any situation where a member of the public, who is engaged in this search for this missing neighbour, will be placing themselves in any danger whatever. However you do raise an important issue and one I would repeat to everyone. Please do not put yourself in any danger, I repeat - any danger whatsoever in the course of this search operation. If it happened, for example, that you were to come across any item which you feel relevant to this search please call the lead member of the search team and under no circumstances should members of the public put themselves in harm's way should that item be in an inaccessible location - for example in deep water. Nevertheless, if any person here has any concerns regarding his own safety or fitness to be involved in this operation then I would urge him to withdraw from the search team now and return home."

Everyone glanced round at the questioner who remained silent. Having ascertained that Mr O'Donlon was satisfied, the garda concluded his remarks.

"Again thank you all for being here. Please quickly join one of the search teams so we can get this search underway."

The milling crowd soon formed up in groups beside their selected garda officer who quickly took control and issued instructions before leading them outside where ten green Toyota jeeps of the Irish army were waiting to transport them to their assigned search location. Everyone was amazed at the organisation in evidence but realised it was only possible because of the high number of army personnel based in the area to protect the border from the IRA and to maintain civil order.

The sandwiches and soup were prepared and dispensed by the ICA assisted by an army field unit at 1pm as announced by Garda McDonald at the morning briefing. All collected again to hear any updates but none was forthcoming. Garda McDonald simply said that the search had as yet not produced any sign of the missing person and would continue. He mentioned how lucky they were with the weather so far but there was rain on the way. "We will reassemble here at 5 this evening or before then in the event of any discovery. Of course each group will be informed of any developments by army radio."

The soup and sandwiches were needed again the next day and people were becoming increasingly disheartened about the possibility of finding Jim Sweeney alive.

Garda McDonald announced at lunchtime on Wednesday;

"Because this man has not been seen alive since Sunday night nor has he turned up elsewhere then there is every likelihood that we are now searching for a body. Because of the level of flood waters in the river and surrounding land I would again ask each group to pay particular attention to the river bank. There are many small inlets and overgrown areas where a body might lie unnoticed. You will have seen that the army helicopter from Finner has joined the search and it will remain on station until an outcome has been achieved. The helicopter will search further afield and will travel the full length of the River Lackan and River Foyle as far as the ocean.

This only underlines the extent of the search area we are faced with. I wish every group good luck in your efforts and I know everyone is very tired but please remain vigilant."

Several searchers were quickly beside the man who had spotted the body and began debating whether to move it before the gardai investigators arrived. The garda officer in charge of the group arrived on the scene. He was soon joined by the army radio operator who reported to the control centre.

"Body of male found at location close to the river bank, approximately two miles east of last reported sighting. Awaiting instructions."

The exposed bluish face showed up against the floating white shirt and the whole body exhibited a considerable degree of bloating, the sign that it had been in the water for several days.

The remains were lifted from the water by four men who floated it to the bank before covering it with the grey army blanket which had been issued to each search team. A radio request brought the army helicopter.

The watching cattle repeated their stampede from the scene when the helicopter landed with a raucous clatter and a stretcher was produced as soon as it landed. The covered body was carried to the helicopter where it was placed on the ground to be anointed by Fr McCarney who had been summoned, as he had requested, when the news of the discovery of the body broke. It was then his job to take the bad news to Mrs Sweeney and her family who were waiting at the home place. The whole family including the mother had been searching since dinner time Monday and neighbours had encouraged them to go home to rest. Garda McDonald went along out of respect and to officially report the event to the family.

The stretcher carrying the body was strapped to a purpose built frame on the side of the helicopter. It was flown directly to Ballyleagh hospital. Dr Fitzpatrick, the deputy coroner, certified the death and had a quiet discussion with Garda Superintendent Mehaffey who had driven the half mile from the garda station to the hospital mortuary on receipt of the news of the discovery.

He had just finished a review of the notes he had made in an interview with the two gardai in the patrol car who had reported to him their version of events on the Sunday night. They had indeed seen a person on the road at around eleven thirty on Sunday night and they wanted to inform the man that he should be wearing a reflective armband in compliance with the current road safety campaign. They turned the car but he had disappeared when they returned to the location where he had been observed. They simply assumed the individual had turned in one of the lanes leading to a farm house in the same area and thought no more about it. He accepted their account but was puzzled by the fact that they had not made any connection between this disappearance on the Sunday night and the man reported missing the next day. He made allowance for the fact that they had been off duty from 8am on the Monday after completing a ten hour shift and were not due to report for duty again until thirty six hours later on Tuesday night.

Both men pointed out they had returned to their respective homes in the mean time and he had no reason to disbelieve that they had indeed taken the opportunity to visit their loved ones on their days off. He was fully aware of the pressure of boredom the officers on this border assignment were under and that every opportunity was taken to get away out of the area. He was also aware they had reported to him as soon as he had come on duty at 8am on Wednesday morning at the end of their Tuesday night shift. Nevertheless he had asked them to have a full written report of the Sunday night sighting on his desk by 6pm on Thursday evening. He also asked them to remain in the station at the end of their shift on Friday morning so that the matter could be fully discussed and the file closed. He reassured them they would receive overtime for any extra hours on duty.

The deputy-coroner and the garda superintendent concluded their quiet hospital discussion and then the garda officer spoke out. "No suspicious circumstances and is it correct that you have seen no unusual or unexplained injuries on the body? "

Dr Fitzpatrick nodded and spoke, "The post mortem examination showed water in the lungs. This proved that the deceased was alive when he entered the water and the conclusion is that death was due to drowning. There were no injuries on the body other than minor abrasions which one would expect on a body washed downstream for two miles in a fast flowing river."

"A tragic accident and of course we will have an inquest later." said the Superintendent.

They both agreed again that all the evidence indicated that the death was due to accidental drowning. A drunken man had stumbled into a flooded river in the dark and drowned. The matter seemed to require no further investigation. The Superintendent spoke again. "For the sake of the family it is best to keep the investigation low key and to return an accidental drowning verdict to head off any suggestion of suicide – to spare the family."

Dr Fitzpatrick and Garda Superintendent Mehaffey nodded several times in assenting unison before shaking hands and going their separate ways.

11 WAKE

At 5.30 pm the November night darkness was fully established when the car, containing Mrs Sweeney and her daughter Marilyn with her husband Damian driving, arrived at Ballyleagh hospital. Convey, the undertaker, was waiting to meet them in the entrance. He had been alerted to be ready for his task by Damian who had been speaking to him earlier. Mrs Sweeney and her daughter were soon engaged in an animated discussion with Convey. They were insisting on seeing the body. Convey kept glancing over at Damian shaking his head in an attempt to involve him in his refusal to open the coffin. A viewing of the body was reluctantly allowed.

The coffin containing the body was wheeled out to the waiting family. The viewing took place in a side room of the hospital mortuary and the mother and daughter wept silently and touched the swollen, damaged face of the man lying there. The undertaker had done his best within the limitations of his art.

Soon afterwards Fr McCarney arrived and blessed the body - again. They said a decade of the rosary as they gazed upon and again touched the cold, swollen, shrouded face of the youngest son. The mother then placed her rosary beads in the whitened, joined hands. After twenty minutes viewing Convey entered the room sniffing and suggested closing the coffin. Mrs Sweeney tried to stop him, she did not want to let her son go but after one long, last look and touching of the face and hands she was lead from the mortuary by her daughter and son in law. Damian turned to speak to the undertaker and the priest who were walking a few steps behind. The sobbing of the two women could be heard echoing from the cold, bare, blue painted concrete walls of the hospital corridor as they walked slowly, arms linked, towards the exit doors.

E d d y   M u r r a y

The undertaker spoke,"We will take the body directly to the church? Better that way- gases from a drowned body."

"No." Said Damian, "Mrs Sweeney wants to wake him in the house tonight and we will take him to the church tomorrow with the burial after mass on Friday."

Fr McCarney nodded. He had spoken about this with Damian who was now the appointed chief organiser.

"All right," Murmured the undertaker knowing that this was going against his wiser judgement. "But the coffin will remain closed."

He opened his eyes wide as if to emphasise the need for a positive response to his implied question. Everyone nodded and agreed to meet up at the mortuary at eight o'clock that evening to accompany the hearse to the family home. The undertaker needed this time to make arrangements for the release of the body.

"There will be no need for me this evening," said Fr McCarney, "but I will meet the remains at the church tomorrow evening at six o'clock and we will have the burial after eleven mass on Friday."

Fr McCarney enquired, "Has anyone been in touch with England?"

Damian answered, "Yeah, they all know he was missing and were planning for the worst. I think they are already on their way by train to Holyhead. I am supposed to pick them up in Dun Laoghaire tomorrow morning at 8am. I suppose it will be my job to break this news to them."

"You'd better get a good sleep, no wake whiskey for you tonight." Replied Fr Mc Carney with a slight smile. "Indeed not, I will be leaving about four in the morning and should be back here about midday."

Damian always enjoyed the long essential drive. He loved going to the airport to collect any visiting Yanks and had even driven to Cork in the fifties when such journeys were considered epic. This was the cause of amazed envy and admiration amongst the local youth many of whom owned a bicycle as the only means of transport and had never left the parish in their lifetime.

In the summer of 1957 Damian had driven his brand new, two- tone green, Vauxhall Victor super deluxe to pick up some US relatives who were arriving by liner at Cobh. This was well before the growth of transatlantic air travel. His love of a snazzy car had not diminished to any considerable extent but he had to tailor his motor to the constraints of his family budget. He was now driving a canary-yellow, mark 3 Cortina with single headlamps and no chrome.

The darkness of a winter's evening seemed a perfect background to this scene of grief-filled weeping. It would not have been at all appropriate if the sun had been shining. Damian drove the car carrying Mrs Sweeney, his wife Marilyn and two of his sons, Edward and Michael as they followed the hearse which pulled out onto the Tirmore road on its way from the hospital to the wake house. By the time they had driven the eight miles to the family home the neighbours were starting to arrive and one or two cars had pulled out to join their cortege on the way. The news had quickly spread as usual in such events but more so in this case because of the extensive search which had gone on since dinner time on Monday.

Loaves, ham, eggs, milk, tomatoes and tins of biscuits were already being carried into the wake house by neighbour women who soon set to making tea and sandwiches for the trickle, soon to be a flood, of people already starting to arrive at the house. Irish people do funerals and grief very well; it's the living that presents the problems. Death creates an aura around the stricken family which lasts at least until the funeral but usually until after the month's mind when the mass of that memorial date is said. Then it is back to business as usual when all the usual assignations come into force and all are relegated from the elevated and sacred place bestowed on them by a death in the family especially the tragic death of a younger person whose time had not yet come. The Sweeney family were now undergoing an experience that is universal. They had just entered a place or state that is occupied at some time in life by everyman. This is the place or state called grief.

"Sorry for you trouble, and - isn't it terrible," followed by a handshake was the expressed formality of shared grief and sympathy from all visitors to the house.

Eddy Murray

Local men were soon helping Damian to clear a bedroom to receive the coffin. The bed was moved to a side wall and covered with a white sheet. Six wooden folding chairs were placed along the opposite wall and a pair of candle sticks and crucifix placed on the embroidered white linen cloth covering the small wooden table which had been brought in from the mother's bedroom.

The candles were lighted when the coffin containing the remains was carried into the house and remained so for the duration of the, closed coffin, wake. Additional chairs and folding tables were taken from the Dreamland ballroom so that the cups, saucers and plates of sandwiches and biscuits could be laid out for the visitors. The coffin was carried into the house by four men who had to manoeuvre it carefully round the corners in the narrow hall. The undertaker stood by and generally directed affairs without getting involved in the actual lifting operations.

A single inquisitive blue-grey pigeon, roused from its night roost by the activity, landed on the street and walked circumspectly towards the door of house as the last of the people entered. Pecking around the street and moving toward the door from where it would have been fed scraps of food in normal times. Rover also circled the crowd assembled around the door and then sat peering into the hallway gleam with his ears hanging low as if it too was aware that things had changed.

Damian's son, Edward, emerged from the open hall door and went over to the waiting dog. He rubbed and patted the dog's head and uttered some words of comfort including 'ah the poor dog, the poor pup' repeated several times. He went back into the house and emerged with the bare bones of a leg of lamb with some choice pieces of flesh still attached. The dog gratefully received the offering and, seemingly reassured, returned to his bed in the shed to deal with the bone. The pigeon had also departed.

Silence had fallen on the assembled family and neighbours because of the enormity and the casual violence of the events which had moved things on to this unfamiliar plane where language was useless.

The coffin was placed on the prepared bed and all in the room joined in the usual sacred mantra - the decade of the rosary which was given out by a neighbouring woman who was a member of the legion of Mary. When the prayers were finished another of the women broke in with an aspiration - Jesus Mary and Joseph pray for us now and at the hour of our death.

All replied, "Amen."

That should have been enough and an excellent point of closure but not so, another woman began:

"Hail Holy Queen, Mother of mercy, hail, our life, our sweetness and our hope. To thee do we cry, poor banished children of Eve: to thee do we send up our sighs, mourning and weeping in this vale of tears. Turn then, most gracious Advocate, thine eyes of mercy toward us and after this, our exile, show unto us the blessed fruit of thy womb, Jesus, O clement , O loving, O sweet Virgin Mary pray for us now and at the hour of our death."

All replied - "Amen."

This did signal the end of the prayers.

Edward, who was aged seventeen did not feel any sorrow yet but did listen to the words of the prayer just uttered. He had heard it repeated nightly, maybe hundreds of times but never did he understand its significance until now. To him it still seemed to express a forlorn hope but it did summarise the general feeling of this moment whatever about repeating it daily. He thought it should be saved for special, extreme occasions such as this. He glanced at the tears streaming down his mother's face and felt a pang of sorrow, not for the deceased but sorrow for his mother and his utter helplessness and inability to do anything to alleviate the tragedy and pain that she was feeling. A miracle was needed but unfortunately there was no miracle worker in attendance.

Thus ended the initial reception of the body of Jim Sweeney into the family home for the last time. Three women remained with the mother and sister beside the coffin, talking softly and repeating things like - "Isn't it awful? - I hope he didn't suffer- God rest him"

All meaningless ejaculations but mostly there was silence and the odd prayer from the mother and sister of the dead man.

The men moved from the hall into the kitchen with an overspill into the scullery. The women got busy making tea. Low conversation was ongoing until Damian spoke out to no one in particular: "You know I think I will head off for Dublin around ten o'clock this evening and I will be able to get a few hours sleep in the car before driving back in the morning."

Everyone seemed to think it was a good idea to travel down now and back in the morning.

Edward had been amusing himself in the scullery watching a dripping tap sending ripples across a full basin of water in the sink. Nothing unusual about that but what had caught his attention were the faint shadows caused by minute reflections of the electric light from the ripples. The shadows from the reflections were sent shimmering across the white wall tiles at the back of the sink. At first he thought it was steam rising from the water but he noticed the water was cold and was pleased that he had identified the source of the emanations. The moving shadows brought him back to river banks and warm summer sunshine through leafy trees when he went fishing with his uncle - the man now very alone in the next room. The moving dappled shadow from light through leaves moving in a summer breeze was something he remembered well. But what he was looking at now was more subtle and exactly like the sunlight reflected onto grassy banks from the smallest ripples left by flies touching down on still water or from the cork bobbing and dipping gently as a fish nibbled at the baited hook below. He was distracted from his dalliance with the theory of light reflection and memories by the talk of travel.

Edward thought it might be a good idea if he went down with his father to Dun Laoghaire to keep him awake. This suggestion was declined because there were four people travelling on the boat and space would be limited. Anyway it was agreed that he would be better staying behind to help out during the wake. There was always something to be done. In fact he was immediately dispatched with his brother to the Dreamland ballroom to get more cups, plates and saucers and to call at the local pub for two large bottles of Powers, 400 plain cigarettes and two boxes of matches. The paraphernalia and hardware for a wake.

So it was that Damian Magill found himself at three in the morning trying to get to sleep outside the Holyhead mail boat terminal in Dun Laoghaire. He poured a cup of tea from the flask into a green mug placed on the dashboard beside the blue, plastic figure of the Virgin Mary. He added milk from a small screw cap bottle. Then he unwrapped a ham sandwich which he also placed on the dashboard beside the teacup before replacing the flask and remaining sandwich in the wicker picnic basket that his wife had insisted he take with him. He had resisted the idea at the time but he was glad of it now.

The white woollen blanket was also useful because the inside of a car becomes very cold especially beside the sea in November. He woke up at 8.30 am to the sound of tapping on the window. He opened his eyes and realised the nightmare he had been in was real.

The four visitors, two brothers and their wives, had arrived complete with brown suitcases and heavy coats. After the briefest expressions of sympathy and shock, all luggage and personnel were inside the car and heading north. Many questions were asked but no information was available apart from the bare facts of the search and discovery of the body. Eventually all settled down to sleep and this condition persisted until the car turned onto the home street shortly before noon.

People were soon milling around the car and the new arrivals were immediately ushered inside followed by their luggage in the hands of neighbours. The mother, now clad in black, soon appeared. Like all Irishmen, the two visiting sons seemed embarrassed by attempting to express sorrow to their mother. The wives had no such problem and were soon hugging Mrs Sweeney with sympathetic utterances;

"Isn't it awful? – The poor fellow – God rest his soul."

Then all entered the wake room in single file. Neighbours respectfully eased their way out of the room to leave space for the visitors.

The coffin was touched, prayers were said and all sat down to talk quietly beside the coffin. Then the new arrivals moved into the kitchen for tea and sandwiches. Sleeping arrangements were discussed so that the new arrivals could get a few hours sleep before facing the removal of the remains that evening.

Eddy Murray

The rain held off for the burial on the Friday and by 12.30 pm all were sitting down to the funeral meal in the local restaurant.

12 QUESTIONS

Questions were being asked as to how the man had ended up in the river but there were few answers.

By all accounts the drowned man left the pub to walk home at around 11.00. It was a Sunday night and it was known that the guards were having a crackdown on illegal late night drinking so the pub had turned everyone out on time.

Nothing else was seen or heard from him until the incontrovertible and definite fact of his body being discovered three days later in the river about two mile downstream from the road. Some neighbours had seen the garda squad car heading out on the same road around the time of the disappearance and everyone was wondering if they had seen anything that would help to solve the mystery.

This was put to the Garda Superintendent in Ballyleagh station on the Friday evening by family members including his sister who had travelled there to see if any more information had surfaced. It was then the family were informed that he had questioned the gardai in the patrol car about their reported sighting of an individual at the entrance to a neighbouring farm house around half past eleven on the Sunday night.

"I have concluded that the patrol gardai were unable to shed any further light on the mystery of the tragic death of Mr Sweeney. The gardai in the car had indeed seen a man on the road around that time and they had turned the car around to tell him he should be wearing a reflective armband but the pedestrian had disappeared by the time they reached the place where they had seen him. They assumed he had turned into the gateway of a farmhouse and thought no more about it."

Marilyn, the sister spoke. "Why did they not come forward when the search was going on? It might have shortened the time before the body was found if we had known where he had been last seen."

The superintendent explained the men had returned home to visit their families around Dublin on their day off and so had not been aware of the news of the search for the missing man until they returned for duty on the Tuesday night.

He continued, "They reported their sighting to me at the first opportunity on Wednesday morning when I came on duty after they had finished their shift. I have had a full discussion with them about this matter."

No one spoke and the Superintendent continued, "I am very sorry for your loss and I can assure you that it is my opinion that Jim Sweeney drowned as a result of a tragic accident and all the available evidence supports this. A very tragic accident."

The men folk nodded and seemed reassured by the words from this high ranking garda officer. Marilyn did not feel reassured at all but recognised the futility of further questioning of the superintendent. As she was getting up to leave she said, "Was Miklan one of the gardai in the squad car?"

The superintendent seemed taken aback that there were further questions on the matter and replied, "If you are referring to Sergeant Mc Grath. As a matter of fact he was but what point are you making?"

Marilyn continued immediately, "I am not making any point but I know that my brother, the man we buried this morning, was afraid of that particular garda. He had a stupid row with my brother over a dog license and he seemed intent on pursuing him about it. He called at our family home several times about it and he was not one bit polite to my mother either."

The superintendent of the gardai seemed slightly surprised when he heard about this dog license affair but was not going to be deterred from his closure of the case. "I have no knowledge of this matter but I fully support my officers in the exercise of their duties in upholding the law. I am sure you would agree that this is our job and the public expects no less."

The sister was not easily deterred and was about to make further comment when the superintendent interrupted, "I can assure you of the integrity of my officers and the fact is they   reported the sighting which may or may not have been your brother at the earliest opportunity and I would urge you to accept the truth of their statements on this matter. Of course you will have the opportunity to raise these matters at the inquest which will be held later. This is a matter for the coroner. I can give you his address and telephone number if you wish to contact him. I would also remind you that you are entitled to be represented by a solicitor at the inquest."

The superintendent seemed relieved, almost pleased with himself and his handling of the meeting as the family trooped from his office.

The family left the garda station and drove directly to the entrance to the lane where the superintendent had indicated the deceased had been last seen - if it was him the gardai had seen on the Sunday night.

The sister spoke,"It was him they saw, this is a small community and everyone knows he was the only one walking the road at that time on that night."

The men were silent and remained in that condition until the yellow Cortina arrived at the spot. They pulled in to the side of the road and got out of the car. All walked back to the laneway and sure enough there was a low parapet that one could easily fall over if you lost your balance or were in a hurry.

 "But it's a wide enough bridge for a car and Jim would know it well." said the sister as the two brothers and Damian were checking the parapet height and saw it came up to the knee as they moved up close beside it to re-enact what might have happened.

"It's possible," said Damian, "that he could have been rushing and overbalanced, could be alright."

Damian moved to the roadside and was inspecting a gap between the parapet and the hedge as he spoke. "You could easily walk in there on a dark night and you would be straight into the river."

"It wasn't a dark night,"said Marilyn, "there was a moon."

Damian interjected,"So are you saying he was trying to get up Dolan's lane to get away from the guards – is that what you think?"

"I don't know what to think, all I know is my brother Jim is dead and mammy will never get over it."

Marilyn took out a hanky and was dabbing her eyes as she spoke, "What is going to happen with the home place now? Who is going to look after our mammy?"

All eyes turned to Damian and Marilyn. Well it was the only possibility because everyone else would be returning to England in a day or two to be back on the building site by the Monday morning.

The family climbed back into the car and were fully engaged for the rest of the homeward journey dealing with more of the practical matters arising from the death.

13 INQUEST

Under section 17 of the Coroner's Act 1962 a formal inquest must be held if the death of an individual, within the jurisdiction of the Irish state, had occurred which was unnatural, unexplained, sudden or violent. In the four weeks since the funeral of James Sweeney there was ongoing communication between the coroner's office and the garda superintendent about the matter. In fact, on the day the body was found, a discussion had taken place between Deputy Coroner Fitzpatrick and Superintendent Mehaffey as to whether there was any need for an inquest at all because the doctor had already certified that death was due to drowning.

The coroner himself was not involved in these discussions because he was a man approaching retirement. He had wrought his medical miracles in the local community for the previous forty years through a haze of regular self-medication with his treatment of choice being ethyl alcohol. Irish peasant society still tolerated such behaviour in its patrician classes. The medical profession were fully paid up and founder members of this class as were the local business owners, the higher ranks of the gardai and, of course, the clergy. All highly respected, above suspicion and untouchable.

At one meeting, which took place on 23 December in the doctor's surgery in Ballyleagh, the superintendent was of the firm opinion there would be no need for an inquest at all because he believed the 'untimely demise of Mr Sweeney' could be construed as an unfortunate accident.

"The drowning could be considered natural since no external agents were involved. There was no evidence of any involvement of other parties." said the superintendent.

"Well ...yes-" said Dr Fitzpatrick in a rare moment of self assertion in front of the law officer. "Indeed the drowning itself might certainly be considered natural but in a way it could also be seen as unnatural depending on how the dead man ended up in the river in the first place."

"Surely you are not suggesting anything suspicious about the death of this man are you?" asked the superintendent with the questioning, indignant tone of a man about to enter a state of impatient irritation.

"No, no indeed not," said the doctor, "Of course not."

However, the doctor was slightly surprised at the degree of involvement of the superintendent and the obvious direction in which he wanted matters to proceed. The doctor simply put this down to operational pressures due to the current political and paramilitary situation in Ireland and to ordinary expediency.

In the end the doctor decided to hold an inquest because as he explained to the Superintendent, "The local paper had reported that an inquest would be held later. Really Superintendent, our hands are tied in this matter. Also there is the family to be considered, they are looking for answers and you can understand they are still in shock, they have just lost their youngest son, they are looking for somebody to explain how their boy came to die in that river."

The Superintendent still saw the inquest as unnecessary and a waste of garda time - time that could be much better spent guarding the border and providing security for the state and he said this to the doctor.

"Well," said the Superintendent, "let us have a damned inquest, but I have no intention of calling my patrol officers to attend and give evidence, they are too busy. I can present their signed statement."

Dr Fitzpatrick was puzzled by this apparent desire to avoid questions about the drowning and about the peripheral garda involvement as potentially the last people to see the dead man alive. This information had become widely known in the local community shortly after the burial. However he dismissed any doubts he might have had and thought no more about it because he, too, was fully aware of the current delicate political situation. However he felt slightly uneasy about the fact that he had been browbeaten by the garda officer. He thought that the superintendent's bluster about state security had achieved its objective of getting the coroner's office to agree that calling the gardai as witnesses would not be necessary.

Further discussion resulted in an agreed date for the inquest which was Friday 6 January 1977. This was in accordance with the legislation as it was outside the minimum time of six weeks which must elapse after the death before an inquest could be held. The venue would be the Dreamland ballroom which both agreed was suitable and in agreement with the requirements of the 1962 Coroners Act.

Superintendent Mehaffey was secretly happy with the date because most of the family of the deceased who might be home on holiday from England, for the Christmas, would have returned to their work by 6 January. This would remove several potential enquiring and complicating minds from the inquest proceedings. The public notice in the paper stated that an inquest into the death of James Sweeney would be held at 9am on Friday 6 January. Location: The Dreamland Ballroom.

Marilyn, the sister of the deceased, remembered that the garda officer had told her that the family could be represented by a solicitor at the inquest. With this in mind she entered the offices of Fee & Son, solicitors in Main Street, Ballyleagh. She had already made an appointment the previous week. As she entered the office she glanced at the gold lettering proclaiming the name of the law firm and their professional services etched on the stained glass in the door. She was ushered in to an inner office where the son, the junior partner in the law practice, sat at his desk and invited her to take a seat.

"First Mrs Magill let me extend our condolences to you and to your entire family on the recent sad loss of your brother."

"Thank you, said Marilyn - I know, I know, it has been a terrible shock to us all."

"Indeed," said the solicitor, nodding sympathetically before continuing, "I understand you are here to see me about us representing you at the inquest. To be perfectly frank I believe the inquest should not be held for months yet until the facts of the case have had time to be fully established, witnesses questioned and so on and also to give your family time to get over the shocking loss of your brother. I don't know what the hurry is, I really don't" he said shaking his head as he perused some documents in front of him.

Marilyn was pleasantly surprised by his level of interest in the case. The expression of sympathy and the reminder of what had happened caused an emotional spasm to rise in her heart and she wished she had made her husband come in with her for support. "Thank you I appreciate what you are saying."

The solicitor continued in a more business like voice because he did not want the meeting to descend into emotion which he always tried to avoid with his clients. Strictly business was his motto. "However we are where we are and the date has been fixed so let us talk about representation. You see the only real purpose for legal representation at an inquest is if there are any contentious issues or matters of dispute. As far as I see this is not the case here."

The solicitor glanced downwards through his half rim glasses and flicked through his notes again. He continued as Marilyn listened intently, looking directly at the suited figure before her. "Forgive me if I am wrong but it has been reported locally that the gardai in the patrol car did indeed see an individual who may or may not have been the deceased. This sighting did occur at a time and location that would have been consistent with the deceased's last journey home."

He paused as he read on; "However when the gardai returned to the location to advise the individual about his safety and indeed to caution him about the current law regarding the wearing of a high visibility arm band he had disappeared."

"Naturally they thought no more about it and resumed their journey. Now I am aware they did not report their sighting until the Wednesday, the day the body had been found, but there was a perfectly logical reason for this. They were away from the area. This lapse may have been significant only because of its effect on the search time. The body may have been found earlier had they been more diligent. However this would not have changed the tragic facts of the case."

Marilyn had heard enough, "I understand all that and you are right but why is no one surprised that a man would take off the road towards a neighbour's house at midnight? Neighbours are all in their beds by midnight on Sundays and Jim would have known that."

The solicitor nodded, "Yes indeed I do see that but it changes none of the facts. This is a much broader subject you are broaching here and one which the inquest will not examine."

"Why not?" Said Marilyn, "I thought the purpose of an inquest was to get at the truth of the death of a citizen?"

The solicitor sat back in surprise at this country woman sitting before him talking about citizens but he said nothing. Marilyn continued, "Did you know that Garda McGrath or Miklan was pursuing my brother over a dog license? I believe they met him on the road that night and surely it is possible that my brother was either pushed into the river by accident or ran from the guards out of fear and fell into the river. In either case the truth should be established. Is that not what an inquest is supposed to do?"

The solicitor interjected, "Mrs Magill, Mrs Magill let me stop you right there. If I **was** your legal representative I am sure you are aware I could not present this type of statement or follow this line of questioning. This is pure conjecture without evidence and indeed you might get away with it because of your emotional state but you must be aware that such an allegation could leave you open to a charge of defamation. The gardai would follow you through every court in the land and it could end up very expensive indeed - for you and your whole family. So there is no point in adding insanity to tragedy."

Marilyn continued, "I know there are no witnesses but the gardai in the car should be questioned by some independent authority that will have access to their written reports and the log of their journey on the night to see if there was any unexplained time-lapse in their journey from Tirmore to Ballyleagh. We know they did not call to any pubs to clear out late night drinkers so there should have been no delay in their journey."

Again the solicitor was amazed at the woman in front of him but his own inclination was to calm everything down. He saw himself as part of the grand alliance with the professional services of Ireland including the Garda Siochana which delivered a stable society across the entire country. "I see your point but I repeat, at the inquest I will be limited to asking the gardai to state what was observed by them on the night and I am sure they will simply state what they have already said to their superintendent. He seems happy enough with their account because I happened to be talking to him just yesterday."

This last piece of information about meeting the Superintendent made Marilyn feel uneasy because she had been of the opinion that the solicitor would be on her side and was even more surprised that he would be discussing the inquest with a potential witness. Despite these misgivings she pressed on, "Do you think a garda patrol car would bother to turn around in the road to advise a pedestrian that he should be wearing an armband? Anyway my mother said Jim always wore an armband and she had even stitched it onto his coat."

"If that is the case," said the solicitor, "then there is a simple explanation. The person seen was not the deceased. I am not being difficult here. I am simply making you aware of what can and cannot be stated at an inquest. It is just like a court of law dealing with facts. So the facts of this case as presented by the gardai are very straightforward and uncontroversial. Circumstances such as the dog license enquiries carried out by the gardai on an earlier date will have no bearing on the hearing and will not be entered as evidence."

Marilyn was about to speak but the solicitor continued, "If there were any evidence of the type you mention then there would be a case for a criminal prosecution or at least a garda disciplinary hearing which may or may not lead to a case for prosecution."

Marilyn felt deflated and frustrated by what she was hearing. She believed the solicitor was speaking the truth but in her gut she felt something was missing out of everything she had heard and was hearing. However she knew she had reached the end of her discussions with the solicitor.

The solicitor spoke again. "There will be no charge for this preliminary consultation but if we were to represent you at the inquest it would cost you upwards of £1000 because we would have to interview witnesses and prepare our statements and I honestly believe that there is nothing to be gained from our presence at the inquest other than as support for yourself and your family. Of course we will be quite happy to represent your family at the inquest if you so wish and request it."

He moved his chair backwards from the table to indicate her time was up. Then he stood up and with outstretched hand he again offered his sympathy. Marilyn did not take his hand and standing up, said, "Thank you Mr Fee, I understand what you have said but I am not convinced."

The solicitor concluded, "Go home and think about it and you have my telephone number if you wish to make another appointment."

The solicitor sat back down and Marilyn made her way from the warmth of the office into the sleeting December cold.

The caretaker opened the Hall at 8.30am in the diminishing morning darkness and switched on a small electric heater close to the table set up for the coroner. The table was sitting in front of the stage with ten wooden folding chairs arranged in front at a distance of about six feet. The deputy coroner arrived with his brown leather brief case at 8.50 and duly set about laying out his papers on the table. He was accompanied by his secretary who had a notepad and pen which she placed on the table in front of her. She tested her pen on a blank sheet of paper and then looked down the hall. "It's damned cold in here." said the deputy coroner.

The secretary just nodded vigorously and hugged herself while wrapping her coat tighter around her perfectly pointed bosom.

Five individuals entered at the rear of the hall and walked to the front where they took their seats. This was the family – the mother, the sister and the son in law and two neighbouring men including Mr Magauran who had discovered the body in the water. Dr Fitzpatrick acknowledged their presence and nodded respectfully towards them. Attention then shifted to the figures of Superintendent Mehaffey and Garda McDonald who had entered the hall and were making their way at a brisk march to the front with their Government issue boots banging on the floor boards. The superintendent spoke to Dr Fitzpatrick and then said hello to the family who did not respond. Garda McDonald gave a sympathetic smile and nod of his head towards the family but did not speak.

The doctor yawned briefly with one finger to his open mouth.Then with his elbows resting on the table he rubbed his hands together before placing them under his chin but not touching it while still vigorously rubbing his hands together.

"Good morning everybody – I expect everyone is here who will be here so we can begin."

It was cold in the hall and the doctor suggested that everyone might benefit by moving closer to the heater. Chairs and people shuffled towards the table and all settled down again to a smile from the doctor, the chairman of the inquest.

He began, "We are here to conduct an enquiry or inquest into the death of James Sweeney of this parish who met an untimely end on Sunday 20 November last. May I, on behalf of the officers of the inquest and the Irish State, extend my sympathy to the bereaved family? Death is always tragic but this one was especially so."

 He paused after this and received a nod in acknowledgement from the three family members present. At this point a black suited figure entered at the back of the hall. This was Fr McCarney who made his way quietly to the front and took a seat. He smiled over at the family and this was returned. They were very glad he had come.

The doctor continued. "I now call Garda McDonald who was the first member of the Garda Siochana to become aware of the missing man. Perhaps Garda McDonald you would please take the oath and outline for the inquest record how you came to be involved in this case."

Garda McDonald stood up, placed his hand on the bible being held by the secretary and read the pledge to tell the truth and nothing but the truth. He then opened his small flip pad and proceeded to divulge his account of events.

"On Monday 21 November 1976 at approximately 2.30pm I was on duty at the public desk in Ballyleagh station when the phone rang and I answered to an individual who introduced herself as Mrs Sweeney, the mother of the deceased, who is present today. She appeared quite calm and recounted to me that the deceased had not been seen since he had left the pub in Glenlackan around 11.00pm on Sunday 20 November last. The deceased lived with his mother and apparently he had not been discovered as missing until he failed to appear for his dinner in his mother's house, his abode, at around 1pm on the Monday. The alarm was raised locally and when it was discovered that he was not to be found at any of the neighbouring houses the decision was taken to contact the gardai."

He continued, "I think that Mrs Sweeney will agree with this. There is also the fact that two gardai in a patrol car passed an individual on the road on the previous night around 11.30pm. The time and location of the sighting indicated strongly that this may have been the deceased. The two officers noticed that the individual had not been wearing a reflective armband so they turned their car around to inform him of the need to wear the reflective band in the interest of road safety and compliance with the law. You will recall there was and is a road safety campaign ongoing at present in an attempt to reduce pedestrian deaths on our roads."

The coroner nodded and made copious notes as did his secretary.

Garda McDonald went on, "When the gardai reached the spot where they had seen the individual he had disappeared. They assumed he had simply called in to one of the neighbouring houses in the vicinity. The two gardai were off on home leave for the next two days so it was not until the start of their shift on Tuesday night that they discovered the facts of the missing man. At the end of the shift on the Wednesday morning they immediately went to their superior officer to report their information and see if it had any bearing on the search. In fact it had no bearing whatsoever because the search was already focussed on the river and the body of the deceased was found on the Wednesday afternoon approximately two miles downstream from the point where the individual had been observed. Later questioning of residents in the vicinity lead me to the conclusion that the individual seen on the road by the two gardai in the patrol car was indeed, in all likelihood, the deceased."

Eddy Murray

"Thank you Garda McDonald." Whispered the deputy coroner as if overcome by the solemnity and emotion of the hearing. By this time quiet sobbing and sighing could be heard from the two women of the Sweeney family.

Garda McDonald proceeded to tell the inquest how a large search party made up of members of the army, the fire brigade, students from the local agricultural college and neighbours were engaged in a two day search culminating in the discovery of the body close to the 'confluence of the Foyle and Lackan rivers' and two miles from the last sighting of the deceased.

The chairman nodded and smiled gravely as the garda officer finished his evidence. "Thank you garda for that very complete account of events and can I on behalf of the coroner's office and the family take this opportunity of thanking you and all involved in the search which was carried out in very cold weather."

Garda McDonald resumed his seat and then glanced sideways at the Superintendent who was looking straight ahead in anticipation of his own contribution. The deputy coroner called the superintendent who stood up, moved towards the side of the table and faced down the hall. After being sworn in he turned to the deputy coroner and spoke.

"Operational matters have prevented the attendance of the mobile patrol officers here today. I will read the statement of the two garda patrol car officers who may have been the last persons to see the deceased alive."

The deputy coroner nodded and the superintendent raised his clip pad with an A4 sheet attached and began,

"As we all know the security of the state is in jeopardy at present as a result of the troubles in the six counties and the overspill into this jurisdiction. As everyone is also aware we have a large force of gardai and army constantly patrolling the border in this sector. On the night in question, Sunday 20 November last, the two officers, Sergeant Mc Grath and Garda Moriarty left Tirmore about 11 pm to begin their Sunday night mobile patrol which would finish at 8 am the next morning. Their statement is as follows."

'At about 11.35pm on Sunday 20 November, just about two miles from

Glenlackan village on the Ballyleagh road we passed a pedestrian who was not wearing a reflective armband. We decided we should inform him of the new national regulations for armbands which applies to pedestrians. We turned our patrol car at a suitable location about six hundred yards further up the road and drove back to where we had passed the man. He was no longer on the road. We assumed he had entered a laneway in the vicinity and we turned our car again and resumed our journey.

We became aware of the search for the missing person when we returned to our base station, on Tuesday evening, after two day's leave but we did not make any direct connection with the individual we had seen. On completion of our Tuesday night shift we realised the possible significance of what we had observed and reported immediately to our superior officer on Wednesday morning. We were interviewed by our superior officer on the same day (Wednesday) and he asked us to submit a written statement.

We do not know how things could have been different if we had realised the difficulties the individual might have been in as we arrived at the scene but we did not have any such realisation so it is useless to speculate. We express our sympathy to the family of the deceased for their loss.'

"This statement is signed by both garda officers and I now submit this statement on their behalf."

The superintendent concluded and resumed his seat after expressing his sympathy and that of every member of his division to the family.

The deputy coroner was about to continue when Marilyn, the sister of the deceased, tentatively raised her hand to catch his eye. He looked at her over his glasses and asked her to continue. In a clear unemotional voice she produced her question. "Which of the two gardai decided to stop and turn the car around?"

The deputy coroner again leaned his elbows on the table with his hands cupped and both thumbs gently caressing the base of his chin. He looked questioningly towards the garda superintendent who was displaying some annoyance at the very notion that any member of the public would have the audacity to ask a question about members of the force or their statement. He snapped out a reply, "I do not have this information at present nor do I see the relevance of the question."

But he quickly recovered control and continued, "However, if the presiding officer believes that this can help his inquest enquiry then we will have to adjourn and I am sure my officers will be able and happy to supply the requisite information."

The deputy coroner nodded sympathetically then shook his head because he did not like the sound of the word adjournment. "Indeed, I tend to agree that it would not provide any material information that might be useful to me in reaching my ultimate conclusions regarding the untimely demise of the late Mr Sweeney."

Then looking towards the questioner he continued, "However I am quite sure the superintendent would be happy to supply you with that information on an informal basis outside this enquiry."

The superintendent nodded his head and uttered one word, "Absolutely."

Looking with a smile towards the lady who had asked the question.

The inquest heard brief further evidence from the family regarding the circumstances of the disappearance. This information was supplied by the son in law Damian because Mrs Sweeney was feeling unwell having contracted some kind of flu that had annoyed her for two weeks past and seemed impossible to shift. She wanted to be at the inquest but was unable to stand and speak.

Mr Magauran, the neighbour man who had found the body also gave evidence. The chairman looked towards Mr Magauran. "Mr Magauran would you take the oath and tell the inquest of your experience?"

James Magauran rose to his feet and was duly sworn in before he began, "I first heard my neighbour, Jim Sweeney, was missing around two o'clock on Monday 21 November. His mother came to our house saying her son had not come home the night before. We calmed her down and told her he would turn up but we were wrong as we all now know. Anyway, everyone knows the story of the search for Jim and it was my luck to discover the poor man's body. Sorry Mrs Sweeney."

As he wiped a tear from his own eye in response to further weeping from the mother, he continued, "Anyway, the rest you know, the body was found lying on its back in about two foot of water. It was hidden by reeds or it would have been found earlier."

He paused before continuing, "Now I know that Jim Sweeney drowned in that river but I will never understand how he got into it. Me and him knew that bridge across the river well and any time we cross it we always stay in the centre for fear of falling in. As for walking into the river in the gap beside the parapet – never. So there you have it. I am puzzled. That's all."

"Thank you Mr Magauran. I have noted your comments and could I on behalf of the inquest thank you and by extension everyone who so readily volunteered to take part in the search for the missing man and who stuck with it until he was found. Thank you."

The presiding deputy coroner continued, "Are there any more persons here present who wish to add to the proceedings?"

Father McCarney stood up and looked around him before speaking, "In my opinion it is a real weakness of this inquest that the last persons to see the deceased alive are not here this morning. I have heard the explanation from the Superintendent for their absence and I accept this. Nevertheless their absence is most unusual and strange to say the very least, would you not agree Superintendent?"

The superintendent rose noisily to his feet with much scraping of metal chair legs on the wooden floor boards and glanced around the group in front of him before speaking.

"The chairman of this inquest has already accepted the signed statement from the gardai in the patrol car and I have already explained the operational demands on my officers as they deal daily with the security situation which threatens this country. We have already agreed that I will supply all relevant information to the family or their representatives on an informal basis after this enquiry closes."

The deputy coroner nodded and looked at Fr McCarney. "Father, is that satisfactory?" Fr Mc Carney paused for a long time before answering. "I really see no reason for the superintendent to become defensive over this. We are all aware of the political violence in the six counties but to use such events to take shortcuts through the judicial system of the Republic of Ireland will prove damaging and counterproductive to good order in the long run. However in the absence of the two witnesses which you as presiding officer have already accepted as satisfactory then I too have no further questions. However I would like my points noted in the account of the inquest proceedings." Marilyn felt like bursting out in applause because she was so uplifted by the intervention of Fr McCarney but she contained her joy.

The deputy coroner moved to his closing remarks, summing up and conclusion. He began, "I will now sum up, declare the conclusion of the inquest and make relevant recommendations - if any."

"I have before me the post-mortem report on the late Jim Sweeney. My examination of the body of the later Mr Sweeney at Ballyleagh hospital on the evening of 23 November 1976, demonstrated to me that death was due to drowning. The body had several non-life threatening abrasions but these could be attributed to events as it moved in fast flowing water over rocks and such like on the river base and banks. The general condition of the body indicated that it had been in the water for several days."

"It is the conclusion of this inquest that the death of James Sweeney occurred at or around 11.30pm on Sunday 20 November 1976. The verdict is death by accidental drowning."

"I now declare these proceedings closed."

He paused before standing up and arranging his papers which he packed into his brief case. He snapped the lock shut and moved over to have a quiet word with the family who were in animated discussion with Fr McCarney.

"Of course I will send you a copy of these proceedings and submit one to be filed in the public records office. Again I am sorry for your trouble."

He glanced sideways and caught Marilyn's eyes looking directly at him –

silent, staring, glaring, he quickly looked away and made his way from the hall.

The Garda Superintendent and his colleague were already in their car outside the hall and about to head back to base and get on with their job of protecting the community.

There was further discussion on the whole affair between the members of the Sweeney family, the neighbour man and Fr McCarney which included the expression of a general feeling of dissatisfaction with the whole inquest and its lack of completeness or investigation of all the events surrounding the drowning. In particular they were astonished by the fact that the patrol car gardai were not present to give their separate account of events on the night and to be available for questions from the family. They felt the inquest had merely been a retelling of the known facts of the case and had not shed any further light on events of that November night. The defensive attitude of the superintendent was remarked on again by Fr McCarney.

The family wanted to get Mrs Sweeney back home as quickly as possible because she was beginning to feel more unwell so they turned down Fr Mc Carney's invitation to join him for breakfast in the local restaurant.

Eddy Murray

14 POSTSCRIPT

All the Sweeney family members, especially Marilyn, were unhappy because they thought their brother had died in circumstances which had not been fully investigated or explained. The inquest was carried out too soon so they could not prepare properly. It was not very thorough and left many of their questions unanswered. He had been last seen by the gardai in a patrol car who did not report this sighting until the search for the missing man had been under way for three days. One of the gardai in the car had an ongoing disagreement with the deceased over a dog license. The family did not feel the account rendered by the gardai was entirely credible because they thought it unlikely that a patrol car would turn around to advise a pedestrian about the necessity of wearing a reflective armband.

According to his mother, Jim Sweeney always wore a reflective armband and in fact she had stitched one onto his coat because she was concerned about his walking the dark roads in winter. However she did accept it may have become detached. The coat was not among the items of clothing found miles downstream along the river bank and handed in to the garda station in the weeks following the drowning. The family suspicions were only added to by the brevity of the inquest which had returned a verdict of death by accidental drowning. However, as the Garda superintendent had expected, the family were indeed relieved that there was no suggestion of suicide which would bring additional shame on the family.

The Sweeney family wanted to know why it was decided between the deputy coroner and the Garda Superintendent that there would be no need for the gardai in the patrol car to attend the inquest. They thought these two law officers should have been required to submit themselves to whatever questions might be put to them in a public examination of events and facts to help shed light on a sudden death. The explanation offered was that they were involved in vital security work in another sector and it would mean a full day off from operational activities. The family considered a single written statement signed by both gardai to be unsatisfactory and unverifiable.

Likewise they thought the advice from the solicitor was seriously sub-standard because it is perfectly possible to question potential witnesses without prejudice or suggestion of any wrongdoing. Such questioning in public could be conducted in an entirely non-accusatory manner to obtain independent accounts from the two gardai. Their demeanour under questioning would give useful information as would the quality and consistency of their accounts or answers to simple questions which could be legitimately asked.

Simple questions which could and should have been asked like: Which of the gardai decided to turn the car around or was the decision mutually spontaneous? Would it be normal to interrupt such an important security patrol for a trivial matter such as the wearing of an armband? Did one of the gardai have an ongoing dispute with the deceased? Had one of the patrol gardai been drinking before going on duty?

The fact that the deceased was probably observed on the road by the occupants of the garda squad car was duly noted at the inquest but there was no discussion as to why, on a cold midnight, a man would divert from his homeward journey and turn in a gateway when he saw a garda car. Had this citizen any reason to fear the garda officers? All these kinds of questions had been put to the superintendent already and he simply repeated what the patrol gardai had told him and said finally – "you don't question the word of a garda officer."

A classic open-and-shut case was the accepted version in the media and in the community. Accidental drowning was the verdict delivered to the family in an official inquest statement signed by the same deputy coroner who had signed the death certificate in the hospital morgue. The statement was brief and contained no details of the proceedings at the inquest itself. No one seemed to think there was any cause to question the verdict or how a man who knew the road and the river very well could simply walk into it by accident on a moonlit night - even if he had been drinking.

The brothers had returned to England a few days after Jim's funeral and Christmas came with all its constructions and preparations to keep one busy. Then, two months later, in February 1977, the mother died having spent the ten weeks since the death of her youngest son in a tear-filled state of depression and grief from morning till night and through the night. The sons all returned for this second family funeral then went back to England to their families. The drowning in November was hardly mentioned as everyone dealt with this latest trouble.

In a moving funeral oration for Mrs Anne Sweeney Father McCarney spoke eloquently about the spirituality of the woman in contrast to its absence in the Ireland of today.

He said:

'The cold February wind is blowing raindrops across the Sweeney family grave today, anointing the headstone with the sacred water. Not made sacred by the blessing of any human hand but innately so because it was part of the creation touched by the divine hand and infused with sacred qualities at the beginning if you care to believe in this type of thing.

Such belief is difficult now because the mind of the modern Irish is a delirious mess of confused thinking where the only real belief is in material possessions. People in Ireland once believed in the sacred nature of all existence down to and including the hard stone in the field. Water was thought endowed with special qualities presumably because of its close association with life itself.

In a direct connection with such ancient customs many women in Ireland, like Anne, still shake holy water on a car before a journey or round a house in a lightning storm. Who would disagree with the idea that this act, intention and touch of these spiritual women makes this water and practice doubly sacred quite irrespective of any words uttered over the water by a priest. Such feelings would now be called primitive and superstitious. They have largely gone from Ireland and taken their spiritual ghosts with them. Still the wind continues to blow, the rain continues to fall and the sun continues to shine to re-create the miracle of the sprouting seed that still happens in this barren place deserted by the human soul. Modern science might yet

Eddy Murray

reach similar conclusions to those ancient superstitions as it gets closer to discovering that all the material things to which we cling so fervently are nothing but an interesting assembly of energy.

Anne was uncomplaining in a life of hardship with many trials. As we all know and remember this has included the loss of her youngest son in tragic circumstance just a few short weeks ago which dealt her a severe blow. Nevertheless the woman we are mourning today still maintained her human dignity and never lowered her standard despite all that life threw at her. She never lost her soul in the true meaning of that phrase. Now, in full awareness of her heroic qualities, let us take her to her rest today beside her late son. Ar dheis De a raibh a anam uasal.'

The mother's death just ten weeks after her brother bore most heavily on Marilyn too. She took to the drink and remained in close association with that inebriant for the remainder of her life.

However, she continued to voice the concerns that caused her to question the garda story. She joined a women's group who, amongst other activities such as drinking tea and chatting, would discuss matters of social concern. This group was formed in the first place to support women who were very worried that a series of actions by gardai in Ireland generally, but especially in Donegal, would suggest that some members of the force were out of control and seemed to consider themselves to be above the law. The group emphasised the need to consider the instability and political insecurity introduced into Irish society by the armed insurrection which was taking place across the border. They recognised that these conditions placed the gardai in an unassailable position as heroic defenders of Irish society in a time of danger, a time when their actions would not be open to the standards of scrutiny and accountability expected in a normal western democracy.

The group went with the sister to look at the place on the road where the deceased had disappeared according to the tardy gardai. They examined the bridge leading up to the neighbour's house where it was assumed the deceased had been heading and noted it was a bridge that was wide enough for a car. The group prepared a report based on their own investigations.

They concluded it might indeed be considered possible that a drunken man could fall over the parapet or miss the bridge on a dark night and walk into the river. But this was a moonlit night and the man was not particularly drunk because at the point where he encountered the garda car he had already walked two of the three miles towards his house. According to the time frame the two mile walk had taken him no more than half an hour which suggested a brisk walking pace. The report mentioned the neighbour who had found the body and who had also expressed his doubts on these matters at the inquest. The real problem for the women's group was the late arrival of the garda information regarding the last sighting of the deceased. The group thought it was surprising that the patrol gardai, even if they were on two days leave, were unaware of a man missing in their sector because the Radio and TV news had been carrying regular reports in an effort to help the search.

By June 1979 the women's group had added further information to their report which was issued as a small pamphlet simply entitled Jim Sweeney (1949 -1976). Marilyn kept informing and updating everyone she met but after an initial burst of enthusiastic support no one seemed particularly interested and even Damian, her husband, got tired in the end. She kept on meeting with the group in an attempt to keep the issue alive.

At many meetings in the following years she could be heard repeating her chorus of questions. Why was it a full three days after the Sunday night sighting before the gardai in the patrol car suddenly remembered seeing someone walking on the road about two miles from Glenlackan village? Why was their information and explanation for turning their patrol car not fully investigated at the inquest? Why did the superintendent form the opinion that the information which his officers could provide would add nothing to the inquest and why did he reassure them there would be no need for them to be called as witnesses for the stated reason that it may or may not have been the deceased they had observed? This latest piece of information had come from the duty sergeant in the station on that night in November 1976. By now it was 1987 and he had just retired.

She was excited to have made some progress even though it was ten years later in July 1987 when the now retired duty sergeant had come forward. He said he had been surprised when he heard about this failure to call himself or the other two garda officers to give evidence at the inquest. He told

Marilyn that disagreement with the superintendent would be a definite barrier to advancement in the force. He explained the motivation of the superintendent whose only interest was in preventing damage to his own career which would have been jeopardised by evidence of any garda misconduct in his division. He went further and said that Miklan and Moriarty were very, very relieved when they were simply transferred to another sector and allowed to continue their patrol work bringing security to the Irish border.

Marilyn's drink habit became more pronounced with the passing years as her own investigations seemed to be going nowhere because she found it impossible to get any official interest in her case. The women's group continued to support her but had moved on to consider wider social ills and were busy arguing for things like contraception in the Republic and had organised several shopping expeditions to buy condoms in the north. In 1990 the group also became involved in the campaign to elect Robinson, the first female president in the history of the state.

Having taken up residence in Aras an Uachtarain - The Presidential residence - the new president placed a candle in the window as a traditional welcome for returning or holidaying members or descendants of the Irish diaspora. Marilyn fell slightly out of favour with the group because she was prone to say things like:

"I doubt if any of President Robinson's children will have to emigrate so the candle is not for them."

Her TD, a woman called Roughlan, listened but in the end dismissed her as a crank when she started saying things she had heard at the meetings - a state which cannot protect its citizens from murder or manslaughter by its police has no law. If the police force is above the law in Donegal, it is above the law across the country and that should worry every man, woman and child in Ireland.

In association with the women's group she issued further press statements which contained troublesome ideas such as: It is considered fundamental that judicial control of the police force can only function in a proper democratic society which cannot be achieved in this divided island.

The slogan at the top of every statement from the women's group read: Quis Custodiet Custodes? Which someone had explained to her as - Who will guard the guards?

Despite Marilyn's best efforts it looked as though the case of the drowning of Jim Sweeney was indeed becoming finally closed after more than a decade without any proper investigation or official interest. The only person to keep the wound open was the sister, the ancient mariner of Glenlackan, who could be heard telling anyone who would listen that the gardai had murdered her brother. As time went by she got fewer listeners and even less as the drink took hold. On one drunken encounter with a group of gardai in a neighbouring village she was threatened with immediate arrest if she insisted on repeating her belief that the gardai in the patrol car murdered her brother or at least were there when he fell into the river.

Her own husband and main supporter had died in 1980 so she had more time to drink and expound her murder theory. The case was finally closed when the lone campaigner died in 2004. However she had lived long enough to read about investigations into garda criminality, corruption and mistreatment of people in Donegal in the nineteen nineties and earlier. The judicial investigations found that certain garda officers, including some at senior rank, were guilty. She wondered if any of the individual gardai so adjudged had been involved in the death of her brother. However by this time she was worn out and could not raise the energy or enthusiasm to organise a new campaign to have the death investigated in a proper judicial process. Instead she ended her days in a confused alcoholic haze.

The family grave of the Sweeney family containing the mortal remains of Jim Sweeney and his mother is marked by a simple, grey granite headstone. No one thought to write their names upon it but this is not unusual in Ireland where emigration or circumstance has taken whole families out of an area. This was not always the case because the graveyard is filled with many fine stone tombs and headstones fully inscribed. The most notable thing is the grandeur of some of these for this was the very type of bare soiled territory which Cromwell had in mind when he consigned the defeated Irish Royalists to a life of hardship, premature death, emigration and transportation or to hell. In keeping with Irish tradition Marilyn is buried in her husband's family plot which is in the graveyard of a neighbouring parish.

Eddy Murray

The Irish state has no interest in preserving Jim Sweeney's name either. Unsurprisingly, a search of the archival records of the garda station yields no information regarding the fact that he had gone missing or that a search had found his body. Surprisingly, the inquest report has also mysteriously disappeared.

Similarly garda pension branch knows nothing. The garda officer who led the search did not exist because no garda officer named A. McDonald appears in their pension records and of course the names of the mobile patrol cannot be found at all at all. Standards of record keeping at Garda Pension branch must be very, very poor indeed. The Irish times in 1997 records the presence of at least one A. McDonald in the force. The report states that, in July 1997, an Inspector *A. McDonald* led a seizure of arms in Co Monaghan. Still the garda pension branch is adamant they have no record of any A. McDonald in the force.

The garda ombudsman's office deals only with complaints about garda behaviour. It has no responsibility for institutional failures. For example it cannot investigate complaints that garda records were not properly maintained at the local garda station or in the central facilities such as the pension branch. Of course the gardai have no responsibility for preserving inquest reports - that is the responsibility of another branch of the Irish 'public service'.

Now it is possible that specific records can accidentally get mislaid or go missing over time but it is a singular surprise to discover that all the records have disappeared. The only evidence that Jim Sweeney ever lived is his birth and death certificate which do exist in the public records.

Three weeks before the Shelbourne meeting with Miklan and his uncle, Minister Paddy Donegan had been involved in a serious constitutional crisis which resulted in the resignation of President Cearbhal O'Dalaigh. The president had decided to act within his powers and used the Supreme Court to test the constitutionality of draconian anti-terrorist legislation which the coalition government had sent to him for signing into law.

Two days later in a speech to an Irish army gathering on 18 October 1976, Paddy Donegan called the president a 'thundering disgrace' and refused to apologise for this interference with the Office. Since no apology was forthcoming from the minister and since The Taoiseach (prime minister) Cosgrave had not demanded his resignation, the president resigned on principle because the government minister had undermined the office of the President of Ireland. Donegan himself was out of his job as Minister of Defence on 2 December, just six weeks after the president's resignation but the next minister simply carried on his policies. The Donegan comment reflected the attitude of the government which was in a state of extreme panic because the IRA was becoming increasingly active and successful in Ireland and Britain. They had assassinated the newly appointed British ambassador, Ewart Biggs, just 5 months earlier in Dublin. There was talk of inside information.

Miklan was duly appointed as the garda - army liaison officer or undercover internal investigator and carried on in that role as Inspector McGrath until retiring in 1998 by which time the large garda security presence on the border had been removed because of the IRA ceasefire and 'peace process' in the six counties. Miklan achieved his dream of owning several houses for rent in Dublin and, now retired, lives for the winter months in his oceanside villa south of Malaga with his mother. He owns a large cabin cruiser which he uses to impress his old colleagues and new friends on deep sea fishing expeditions. He also provides security personnel for several clubs in Estepona and always takes an annual two week holiday in Thailand. Miklan never married.

Garda Moriarty retired with the rank of garda. He never sought and was not offered promotion despite his excellent record and good relations with the public. He married in 1982 and still lives in Dublin with his wife. He has four children all of whom have now set up their own homes. He still regrets his failure to act on principle on that Sunday night in November 1976.

******

Eddy Murray

Footnote

After Marilyn's death the women's group issued a brief statement dated June 2005. It had the usual heading:

Quis Custodiet Custodes.

We deeply regret the death of our esteemed member Marilyn who has been tireless in the pursuit of truth and justice in the case of the untimely death of her brother in 1976.

Judicial inquiries into serious garda misconduct in Donegal, in the years after the drowning of Jim Sweeney, found that some members of the force, at all ranks, have been involved in serious criminal activity and extreme harassment of local people. The inquiries uncovered abuses of power that would have been worthy of the police force in the worst banana republic. Was Jim Sweeney another victim of such criminal gardai?

The final conclusion must be that the gardai remain a police force without the proper control of an independent regulatory body. The ombudsman has power to investigate individual cases of garda misconduct but not institutional failures which will recur because no essential changes have been made to the structures of this police force or its various branches which judicial inquiries have found wanting. The criminal classes must be very relieved because an overpaid, superannuated, inefficient, lazy, corrupt and demoralised police force is exactly what they need to survive and prosper. One is always reminded that the Irish police force, the gardai, is badly led and some members lack professional or social responsibility as demonstrated by their adoption of the 'blue flu' blackmail in 1998 to achieve their own selfish financial objectives.

The Irish statutory authorities, political classes and media have never been slow at aping English practices. Maybe it is now time to do a little more useful aping by looking at English or other European models of policing and adopting some of their regulatory systems.

Eddy Murray